BOOK **4** OF THE WITCHBOUND SAGA

the NATURE of MAGIC

NATALIE GIBSON

Livonia, Michigan

Editor: Hannah Ryder
Proofreader: Anna Heiar

THE NATURE OF MAGIC
Copyright © 2022 Natalie Gibson

All rights reserved. No part of this publication may be reproduced, distributed, or transmitted in any form or by any means, including photocopying, recording, or other electronic or mechanical methods, without the prior written permission of the publisher, except in the case of brief quotations embodied in critical reviews and certain other noncommercial uses permitted by copyright law. For permission requests, please write to the publisher.

This book is a work of fiction. The characters, incidents, and dialogue are drawn from the author's imagination and are not to be construed as real. Any resemblance to actual events or persons, living or dead, is entirely coincidental.

Published by BHC Press

Library of Congress Control Number:
2021944340

ISBN: 978-1-64397-277-0 (Hardcover)
ISBN: 978-1-64397-278-7 (Softcover)
ISBN: 978-1-64397-279-4 (Ebook)

For information, write:
BHC Press
885 Penniman #5505
Plymouth, MI 48170

Visit the publisher:
www.bhcpress.com

ALSO BY
Natalie Gibson

Witchbound
For the Love of Magic
The Dying Art of Magic
The Magic Number

Multi-author Anthologies
In Creeps the Night
A Winter's Romance

To all those lucky enough
to know the pull of family land.

THE NATURE OF MAGIC

ONE

Barefoot and naked, Tara Kay ran through the woods, her woods, as fast as her short legs would carry her. Nighttime darkness fell so long ago that it was technically already tomorrow. At least she wasn't in high heels like an idiot girl in a horror movie. She felt a laugh bubbling up, but she stifled the sound. The trail mix of drugs she had taken was making it hard for her to think clearly or remember what she was running from, but the noises coming from behind were reason enough to keep running. The men's heavy feet and taunting words pushed her forward. The last of the branches scratched at her bare skin as she broke free and tumbled into the clearing.

Directions played on a loop in her hazy head. *Just get to the tree. Your tree will save you. Reach your guardian and you will be safe. Just get to the tree. Your tree will save you. Reach your guardian and you will be safe.* The voice was female, but it wasn't her own. She felt sure she had heard it before, but it was never this clear. She tried to remember when it was; her high made it impossible to reason. She shook her head in an effort to clear her mind.

The movement disoriented her, and she fell. She panted, the cold of the earth soaking in. The ground cover where she'd landed was soft but that could be her mind playing tricks on her. It felt like a patch of clover but, as cognizant as she was, she could very well be laying on a bull nettle. The voice urged her forward again. *Just get to the tree. Your tree will save you. Reach your guardian and you will be safe.*

She could see her tree straight ahead, silhouetted against the night sky. The waxing gibbous moon, fat with light, watched it all from its position a little to the right. With her dilated pupils, Kay could easily see her path. She'd made this same trek a thousand times but never under this level of duress.

Hearing her three pursuers break through the edge of the forest, Kay knew she had to run, but her body wouldn't respond. Ashley Stout, her on-again, off-again boyfriend, spotted her ultra-white skin in the near full moon's light and pointed her out. His half-brother, Jackie, made an obscene comment about her being face down all sprawled out, waiting for them. Will still hadn't said anything, but when she looked back, their eyes met. He was silent but hungrier for hurting her than his friends. She and Will had a history neither of the other two knew about and it included her turning him down flat.

Hurry, the woman said in Kay's mind. Kay thought about just lying there and letting them catch up to her. She was rolling and tripping so hard that what they wanted to do with her might even feel good. She hadn't liked the *way* Ashley proposed it. He had given her to his half-brother and friend to do with what they liked. He'd said that it was to prove that she was indeed his. "A man can't give away something that doesn't belong to him, can he?" She had bolted not then but later. She had been kissed and caressed and undressed by them, seemingly agreeing to the proposal. She ran because of something in Will's eyes. He was going to hurt her, not if, but when he got the chance.

Then just as Will was close enough for her to hear him panting, she was up and running. She hadn't decided to get up. The ground under her had seemed to move, heaving her up. Behind her the three cursed and fell, claiming the ground had moved on them too. Only it had worked against them when its motion had helped her.

Her bare feet found better traction than their booted ones. She had country feet, as she called them. They were used to the hot asphalt, sharp gravel, poking stickers, and rough sand and dirt. They were also ugly as sin, but she didn't let it bother her. She liked having contact with the earth.

The path was clear. She ran. Just two steps before she would make her leap to the lowest branch, her toe caught on a vine that she would have sworn wasn't there before. Her momentum propelled her torso forward but her foot, trapped by the vine, took her down. She had just enough time to get her hands up, but not the strength to truly catch herself. Her face hit a root poking out of the ground at the base of the tree. She saw stars. Her lips, pinched between her teeth and the hard root, were pulverized. Her mouth filled up with blood and she was certain that she would lose a tooth or two.

The blood, looking dark but without color in the night light, dripped onto the root, staining it. Thankfully Tara Kay didn't lose consciousness. She got up quickly and made the familiar journey from branch to branch until she was in her favorite place, a high fork in the massive trunk that had a dip where she fit perfectly. She straddled it and leaned her head back to rest on one side of the fork.

She didn't close her eyes and as she sat staring at the bark, the drugs in her brain tricked her eyes into seeing a face there hidden in the tree's protective covering. She leaned forward and gave the hallucinogen-made mouth a bloody kiss in thanks. The three would-be rapists had reached the tree but were finding it impossible to climb. Her blood colored the imaginary lips, making them more convincing than before. Kay leaned back, stretching her arms up over her head. Green leaves tickled and caressed her back, sides, neck, and arms. She imagined a wooden tongue darted out to lick off the crimson and then the face disappeared.

She stared up at the moon peeking down at her amid the branches, and she enjoyed the caress of her tree. Her guardian was more alive now than ever. Drugs very rarely gave her the religious connection to nature and others that her friends reported, but something was obviously different about the cocktail she'd taken tonight. As she peaked, Tara Kay became certain that the tree, her tree, was not only alive but a thinking being. The voice she'd heard tonight and other key times in her life was the great mother earth and this tree was her son.

The ruckus below crescendoed and then tapered off as if she were being removed from it. She heard a growl and shouting. Perhaps a wild animal had scared Ashley, Jackie and Will off, but she couldn't spare a thought for them now because the dose was taking over any and all thought. The bark beneath her and the branches above her changed.

This was some hallucination, and she gave herself over to it. The face was back, and she was being carried by a giant man. Her thighs were on either side of him, resting on his hip bones instead of the scratchy hard plant. She crossed her ankles behind his back and eased herself down to the tip his waiting erection.

The branches she nestled in became his arms wrapped around her and the leaves his fingers on her back. His grip tightened and pulled her torso close to his. She rested her elbows on his shoulders and brushed the hair away from his face. She traced his handsome features with her fingertips. "My beautiful guardian," she said in a lover's whisper.

He said something in a language she'd never heard and didn't understand but it ended in "Sin-eese." She was struck by the quality of his voice. It was pleasant but rough and unused. A rusty virtuoso of a voice he had, like Pavarotti after breaking a yearlong vow of silence. It was more than that, otherworldly even. It pleased her to no end. Sexy, masculine, soothing and musical: it was a proper voice for an oak tree and a magnified version of everything she preferred in a lover's voice.

Then with hand at her waist and one palming the back of her neck, he pulled her down into a kiss even as he shafted her. The kiss was something unlike any before it. Soft but firm, asking and taking, needy but confident all at the same time, he kissed like he'd been drowning and she was air. He devoured her mouth, removing any trace of blood from her collision with his root. His hungry mouth managed to distract her from the fact that she was now humping a tree in a drug-induced vision. She laughed into his mouth and he swallowed that up too. She lifted herself and then lowered back down around his shaft. Sure, she'd have scratches and splinters where the sun don't shine but even that wasn't a deterrent. This was her tree come to life just as she'd always wished it would. The pull was too strong to resist; she had to be with him like this.

She rode him slowly, trying to commit so many details to memory. She needed to retain this even after the delusion ended. Kay could feel every ridge and vein in his cock, the biggest she'd ever had inside her. It stretched her canal in the most satisfying way. Her skin tingled everywhere they touched: the backs of her arms on his shoulders, her thighs on his hips, the tips of her breasts on his chest. The tingle wasn't the only thing that seemed alien to her fuzzy brain. He was hot. Seriously hot. Like a person burning up with fever. His hair was unbelievably rose petal soft and looked green in the moonlight. He was at least seven and a half feet tall and built like a linebacker. His facial features were perfect, and his skin was without flaw. He was covered in a vine-like tattoo with conical flowers that were reflected in the moonlight.

But his eyes! His eyes overshadowed all the other pleasant oddities. They were practically glowing. They were like jewel-cut crystals or opals, facets catching the light and reflecting it back. She could see herself in them and she studied her reflection too. She didn't see any of the imperfections that usually plagued her thoughts when she looked in a mirror. She was beautiful, leaned back rocking herself up and down. Her own hair was green and straight in a shoulder length bob. Her skin looked smooth and creamy white. She could see the blue veins and pink arteries just below the surface. She had tiny pink nipples set high on round full breasts, a narrow ribcage and hips.

With one hand he held her up, aiding her rhythm. The other slowly explored her body. He slid it over her shoulder and then up over her throat, thumbing her pulse for a moment before sliding down over the swell of her breasts, flat stomach, and hip bones before coming to rest at the place where their bodies joined. The sensations were too intense, and Tara Kay stopped her movements to experience them.

He put his forefinger and thumb between her outer and inner labia, slipping up and down her folds that were stretched to the max by his invading member. Each time he reached the top and his fingers met on her clit, he rolled and squeezed it. Kay let her head fall back and she closed her eyes, but she snapped to attention when his dick moved inside her.

The man hadn't moved; his hips weren't thrusting, but it was moving inside her. It was rolling, almost fingering her most sensitive interior point deep inside even as his hand toyed with her most sensitive exterior spot. Then it began to move faster and faster she had no option but to climax. It was *vibrating* inside her, for goddess' sakes! Wave after wave of warm pleasure washed over her and her muscles clamped down on his pulsating penis.

So quickly they barely seemed to move, he turned her, and she found herself on all fours in the soft grass. He never stopped stimulating her clit but was now also pounding her pussy from behind with his magical, somehow mechanical, member. It felt so exquisitely delirious, she fisted the grass and tried to stay conscious. She felt his free hand on her shoulder, steading her for his hammering, then it slipped down to trace designs on her back.

It took a second before she remembered her tattoo and realized he was tracing the picture of her tree there. It was a massive back piece that had taken four sittings, four hours each. It was done from a photograph her grandmother had taken of Kay on the day she was first able to climb to her favorite spot. In it, Tara Kay was perched high, almost hidden by its branches and leaves, but her face was visible as she grinned at the camera in triumph. Kay shared so many of her milestone moments with her tree that she wished this photo was from when she was older, but it had been the only photo ever taken of her in the tree.

He hunched over her and his tongue replaced his fingers. His breath was warm on her back as his moist mouth painted the picture all over again. His pumping never stopped, and she felt she'd been coming for hours. He wrapped his arm around her stomach and brought his kisses up to her shoulder. Kay heard the woman's voice again. It said, "Give him permission to take what he asks." He nipped at the place where shoulder met neck and she angled her head away, giving him access to her throat.

Tara Kay felt a sharp pain as he bit her, but it passed quickly into ecstasy. Her hallucination has taken an unexpected turn, but she was willing to follow whatever path it took. It, so far, had only led to pleasure. She didn't need the woman's urging to accept what he offered her next. His arm slid up to fondle her breasts for a moment as he finished sucking at her neck. Then he wrapped his muscled arm around her shoulder and brought his own wrist back to his mouth. When he placed it in front of her face, she could see the bite mark. A few drops hit the ground before she latched onto the pricks.

She didn't have time to wonder where the pillow below her came from. She took her first draw from his open vein, and his cock jerked inside her. His heartbeat pumped blood into her mouth even as his orgasm spurted against her cervix. She lost all concept of time and space and all thoughts of reality versus dream. She swallowed his essence gulp by gulp and as the darkness took her, she heard the woman's voice again.

The great mother earth spoke with two voices in two languages. *Bring her through Me and We will make her as you are.*

TARA KAY woke to the sunlight on her face. She was on her side and a man's arm was draped over hers. She stayed still. She could remember waking up several times throughout the night. Each time she'd reached out to him, he'd been there. Her guardian. They'd had sex more times than she could count, each one blurring with the one before and the one after until it was just one memory. It was one of total bliss and total abandonment.

She was slightly embarrassed to look her new lover in the face. What if he wasn't what she'd imagined. What if he was some crazy homeless man who took advantage of her drug-induced euphoria. Well, not all of it had been her imagination. The finger tracing her tattoo was real enough. She might have imagined his evolution from tree to man, but his existence was not in question. He was a real live man. When he spoke, her fears were laid to rest. That voice alone was enough to get him into her bed, even if he was a hobo.

"*Darisam baltu oren.*"

He wasn't speaking English. She was going to need to see him, if she was going to figure out what the hell he was trying to say. She gathered her courage and turned. She was not disappointed. He was gorgeous, a real heartthrob. He rested on his bent elbow and she mirrored his position to study him a bit. As she watched he, and the world around him, started to glow. Those were some drugs last night, she thought. She'd had the "sparkle" after a trip before but never like this. Everything looked so alive, especially the man beside her. Several things about him jumped out at once. He wasn't as giant as she'd thought last night. Though he was clearly pro-football player sized, he was just a large man, not a colossus oak. His hair was green, though a shade darker than hers, and his tattoos, which covered every inch of his body, were of vines. The vines were covered in leaves, not morning glories.

He gestured to himself and said again, "*Darisam baltu oren.*"

"Oren? Are you trying to tell me your name is Oren?"

He propped himself up on an elbow to look down at her. She was at once distracted by the curve of his arm muscles. She watched helplessly as her hand reached out to trace the lines of his chest. Again he gestured to himself and then made a sign of "tall." "*Darisam baltu oren.*" She tore her gaze from his form and put her attention on his face. He gestured to her and said, "*Ma darisam baltu.*"

"I get it. Hello, Oren." She gestured to herself. "*Darisam baltu,* Tara Kay."

He seemed very relieved. "Tara Kay, *darisam baltu.*" He said her name like all one word, and it had a weird accent on the wrong syllable, TeRAkay. She liked it. She smiled at him and nodded her head. He leaned over and kissed her. It was a soft pressing of his lips to hers, no more. He pulled away only far enough to see her better. He traced her eyebrows, cheekbones, nose, and mouth with his thumb. He started talking but Kay couldn't keep her mind on his words long enough to figure them out. She was hungry.

Seriously hungry with a capital H.

"I'm starved. You?" She made the universal sign for eat. Then showed him her teeth, making a movement for biting and chewing.

He smiled. Good gravy, he was adorable when he smiled. He had lines like parentheses around his mouth and a dimple outside those. He bent and kissed her again, but this one was all passion. Kay allowed it because he was so damn good at it, but when he moved on to her chin and neck, she pushed at him. He clearly didn't understand.

Confused, he pulled from her and furrowed his brow in question. Was it possible for every face a person made to be more attractive than the last, she wondered. She sat up and then stood, holding her hand out to him. Her move had brought his face close to her privates. He stared at the junction between her legs. She thought she even saw him lick his lips before he put his hand in hers. He stood without any help from her, though he kept her hand. He brought it up to his mouth and kissed her knuckles. Each touch sent a little shiver down her spine, into her stomach and a little further south. She couldn't help but notice his erection. He was hungry too, but not for food.

Tara Kay looked around and tried to get her bearings. They were west of the trailer and her tree, not far from the orchard and the old, condemned house. She turned and started to run, pulling him along. She could not remember ever feeling so good. The wind on her face and naked body was stunning. Her hair, where it touched her shoulders, tingled in a most pleasant way. She could feel every strand. The grass where she ran had never felt so soft. She laughed out loud.

They reached the grove quicker than she expected. They walked through the garden and she showed him all his options. There were trees bearing apples, peaches, plums, pears, figs and even avocados. Low ground-hugging plants and bushes bore blueberries, blackberries, strawberries, and melons. Sweet and regular potatoes grew underground as well as the lesser-known taro, but they needed to be cooked before eating.

She enjoyed the way he looked at each plant. She was proud of this place though she had never showed it to anyone other than Mamaw and Papaw. She was glad she could show it to him and happy he seemed impressed. Kay had started this garden quite on accident when she was five, so it wasn't more than twenty years old. She knew that her present company couldn't understand her, but she spoke to him anyway. She told him all about each plant and how it had gotten its magical start here.

She told him she was a witch, an elemental earth witch, from a long lineage of witches. Her mamaw had made offerings of milk and honey to the great mother earth every year at planting season until the year of her death. Sometimes her prayers were answered and sometimes not so much. Kay's offerings were always answered with rewards because she made offerings of her own blood.

She paused to look at Oren. She hadn't told many about her secret, and even though he didn't speak English, she was worried how he might react. He was watching her intently. She told him again that she used her blood to speak to the great mother earth to tell her what was needed.

He nodded that he understood. When she lifted an eyebrow in disbelief, he lifted her arm and pointed to the greenish blue vein that was most often tapped for blood donation. He said, "*Mu gishtil ina sinnis ina ummum zumru warki sessu sessum-esrum*, TeRAkay."

She smiled and shrugged. His was the oddest language she'd ever heard. She had no idea where he was from. He kissed the very same spot, where her pulse was so close to the surface, and her heart skipped a beat. She almost missed a step before she could start her story again.

TARA KAY Woods hadn't had the best childhood. She knew people who'd had it worse, but she knew more that had had it better. Her parents hadn't abused her, but she suffered great neglect. She knew now that they couldn't help it. They were drug addicts, completely strung out on heroin by the time Kay had been born.

She only survived infancy because of her older siblings. She owed her life to her siblings, people whose names she didn't know, but that was another story. She wanted to tell Oren about the garden and her magic, not regale him with tales of neglect and loneliness. She rushed forward through the intro of her narrative.

The real-life threatening problem with having junkies for parents is that they don't eat. They don't even think about eating. They certainly don't plan meals and go grocery shopping. One day in the summer after she'd turned five, she was so hungry that she tried something truly desperate and extreme. She cut her wrist with a sharp rock and sprinkled her blood throughout a clearing in the woods near her family home. She sang and begged for help. She needed a regular source of food. She had seen her mamaw make offerings of milk and honey to the great mother earth before the planting season every year and her garden always made. The milk and honey were collected by Mamaw's own hands because she said the earth required a personal sacrifice before a reapable reward was returned. Young Tara Kay had no way to till or fertilize the ground, no seeds to plant, no knowledge of how things were grown. She needed the food now with no prep work. She needed a miracle. Her sacrifice had to be greater than that of her grandmother's.

It worked. Better than her five-year-old brain could ever have imagined it would.

She didn't know how long she had slept. She'd just passed out on the ground from the blood loss. She prayed as long as she could before the darkness took her. When Kay woke up, she found the garden much as it appeared now.

Tara Kay gestured around her at the mature trees and producing plants of the grove, showing them to Oren. "I ran around gobbling up one of everything, with no thought for the dirty gash in my fucking wrist. It wasn't bleeding anymore. In fact, it had some type of wilderness bandage over it. I tore the plant material off and looked at it. It'd scabbed over and didn't seem infected. I know now that the leafy bandage was from a plant with a very high antiseptic content in all its parts. All I knew then was a woman's voice had come out of my blood-starved mind and instructed me on making the poultice, bandage and tourniquet. That was the first time I heard her."

Oren nodded as if he understood. "*Kiyahwe nisme ma mala bat nisme* Oren."

"Sure, whatever. From then on, whenever I needed something, I just pricked a finger. Just a drop usually worked. Not until I started growing drug substitutes did I really need to make blood offerings again. There is always something growing here. It's not like the sacred fig grove of the Daughters of Women that grows fruit all fucking year. That's pretty damn creepy if you ask me. My grove follows the cycles of the seasons but there is something to eat for every season, and the plants, even the ones that would normally be annuals, grow food every year and live through their off season. You're lucky to be seeing it at the beginning of summer. Almost everything is producing. We've got our pick today."

TWO

"Good choice! You've never had a peach as delicious as mine. I guaran-damn-tee it." She ignored the hungry stare that said he was thinking of her metaphorical peach. She was probably just projecting—after all, he couldn't understand her. She selected the biggest, ripest, most perfect peach she could find and plucked it. She held the golden red peach out for him to take. "Here you can have this one. It's a good one, I promise."

He stared at her.

So much for him understanding her. She got close enough to put it in front of his face. "Go ahead. Take a bite." She held it to his mouth as he gingerly sank his teeth through its fuzzy velvet skin and into its yellow meat. His eyes went wide at the flavor and he chewed slowly, never taking his gaze off her.

She had a bite. It was riper than she'd thought, and the juices dripped down her arm and chin. She stared at the fruit in disbelief. This was the best fucking peach she'd ever tasted. It was head and shoulders above anything she'd ever had and she, herself, had grown some pretty amazing things in this place. Before she knew it, she had taken a second bite and a third.

Its flavors were so complex. It was sweet, but it was also slightly sour and acidic. It was deliciously and disgustingly delectable all at the same time. She could taste the dirt this fruit had pulled its nutrients from, the family land she loved so much. She knew by its taste that it had grown during a dry season, struggling, but that the earth had supplied the flesh. There was a hint of something else there, too. The slightest bit of syrupy sweet rot just starting. She took another bite. She could taste herself in the fruit. The blood she'd shed there all those years ago was still flavoring the fruit. She had never tasted that in her fruits before. It was more like she had never really tasted anything before now. The peach wasn't different; she was.

"TaRAkay." His beautiful voice brought her out of her mental ramblings.

She held the peach out to him. He wanted some. She looked at her hand. The peach was gone. She was holding a pit out to him. She tossed it down and turned to the tree to pick another for him. She reached up to grab one and Oren stopped her arm.

Oren held her by the elbow, then slowly licked all the sticky sweet nectar off. Carefully, he cleaned her forearm from elbow to wrist before moving on to palm and fingers. Kay couldn't believe what was happening. She was in some kind of fantasy. Every experience, every sensation today was enhanced to an almost painfully pleasant level. When he placed kisses on each of her fingertips, she dropped her head back and stared at the sky, convinced she'd see two moons or flying pigs or something.

Her move gave Oren just the offering he wanted. He slipped closer, lapping at a drip on her neck. She wrapped her arms around his shoulders as his mouth worked wonders on her throat. The way he was pulling on her, she was going to have one hell of a hickey, but she didn't care. He lifted and then slanted his head, covering her mouth with his. He was devouring her just as she had hungrily eaten the peach. She tasted herself again, her blood, in his kiss. I must be tasting the peach, she thought.

He continued to make love to her mouth as his hands roamed over her hips, waist, and backside. She loved men's hands, slightly rough and callus. They made her feel delicate and soft. She explored the hard muscles of his shoulders and arms.

His hands in her armpits, he lifted her easily and set her on a strong thick branch of the fruit tree. It was thick enough to hold her weight but not the size of a seat. He hooked her ankles around his elbows and added his hands to give her a bigger, softer area to sit. When he spread his arms her legs went with them, and she realized what this position was for. His face was level with her peach. She had eaten his all up and now it was his turn.

There was no nuance, no easing into it. He just put his face against her and went to town, like she was the most delicious thing he'd ever had on his lips. Oh, those lips. They were casting some kind of spell on her. It wasn't like the perfunctory cunt licking she'd gotten from other men, nor the ones she saw in porn. He devoured her up, not caring about the noise he was making or how it looked. He sucked her clitoris into his mouth and she almost lost her balance. When he used his teeth and tongue to bang out intricate Morse code, she gasped and flailed her arms out. She held on to the branch above her as the feeling of falling slowly overtook the heavy need in her.

With barely a buildup, her orgasm took her. She exploded with an internal fireworks display that stunned her. She came to with the sounds of Oren making out with her blossom, slurping up everything her body had to offer. She realized then that she'd never had a man go down on her who knew what he was doing. Oren was no beginner. This man knew his way around a pussy. She relaxed, letting him handle her weight, and just soaked up the ripples of the afterglow.

But Oren wasn't finished with her body yet. As soon as he lapped up every wave of her climax, he had her on the cusp of another. As Kay shattered for the second time by the magic of his mouth, she wondered if this session was for her or for him. The look on his face, when she had use of her vision, said that he was enjoying it every bit as much as her.

KAY RAN in the kitchen entrance of Dinner Diner where she worked during the day. She hung her purse on her hook, tied on an apron, and tucked the order pad and tiny pencil into its pocket. She waved at the cook, who was looking at her in opened-mouthed wonder. "*Hola*, Marcos!"

She peaked through the circular window into the dining room. She was only a few minutes late, but Margarete had her hands full. The other waitress was running around trying to keep up, but every table was occupied. That was more than one staff member could handle even in this small venue. Ashley, Jackie, and Will sat in Kay's section. Damn it!

She straightened her waitress dress and checked her hair and makeup in the reflective surface of the kitchen doors, but she hated herself for doing it. She didn't want to care what Ashley thought of her, especially after last night, but she did. She wanted him to want her even if she would never want him again. She wished that Oren had come with her. It would be easier to face her ex with Oren around.

She had slapped on some makeup in the car ride over but hadn't been very careful. It was hard to see in the blurry reflection of the metallic door, but she could tell it was good enough. Better than that, she looked really good. Lips shiny pink and plump, eyes adequately lined and accentuated with long black lashes, and every green hair on her head in place, Tara Kay bumped the door with her rump. She backed into the room and spun around, grabbing up the carafe on the way by.

"Sorry I'm late, Margarete! I lost track of time." She called out. The room that was bustling with activity and noisy with friendly clamoring was now quiet. All eyes were on Kay.

She moved around the room warming up the coffee of every truck driver and local alike, hitting Ashley's table last. She set the empty carafe down. "What'll it be?" she said, pretending not to notice who it was. When no one answered she countered, "Not ready yet, got it. I'll be back around in a few minutes," and tried to walk away.

"You gotta be shitting me," Ashley stammered out. Will reached out and grabbed her by the wrist. He jerked his hand back as if she'd stung him.

Tara Kay sat at the empty spot of their four top and let them have it. She said quietly through gritted teeth, "You three assholes think that you can try to…force me and then show up to my workplace like nothing happened? We were all high, I get that, but no amount of drugs is an excuse for chasing me naked through the woods! I said no. No means no. You are not welcome in my home and as soon as I have time to talk to Mr. Glenn, you won't be welcome here either. Choose your meal carefully because it'll be the last one I serve you." She stood and realized they hadn't moved or made a sound since she started talking. She had kept her eyes averted the whole time.

Kay really looked at them for the first time. The small gang was staring at her like she was a leper. They were ghost white and sweaty. Ashley's arm was in a sling and a pair of crutches leaned against the wall behind Will's chair. They all had scratches and lacerations covering their arms and faces plus some type of rash that looked like poison oak. Jackie's right eye was so infected that he couldn't open it. "What the fuck happened to you three?" she asked in a lowered voice. This was a family restaurant, and she got in trouble a lot for her love of using the f-bomb.

No one answered her question. Will swallowed audibly and Jackie started to visibly shake. Their condition made Kay think about how she must look. She glanced at her own arms, searching for the scrapes that should mirror theirs. Her skin was smooth as a baby's butt. She reached up to feel her mouth. She had tripped and fallen, busting her mouth against a tree root, hadn't she? She ran a finger on the inside of her lips but there was no swelling or ridges that spoke of healing damage. Her teeth were all solid and in place. No wiggle at all. Weird.

The bell jingled when a new customer opened the door. Ash knocked over his chair in his hurry to stand. Will's squeaked on the linoleum and a mixture of cursing and prayer poured from Jackie's mouth. Margarete said, "Oh, no you don't. Handsome or not, no shoes, no service, buddy. Read the sign."

Kay looked up to find Oren standing in the entrance looking around like the dirty diner was the most magnificent thing he'd ever seen. His eyes were wide and his mouth hung loose. He was barefoot. The clothes she had given him were way too tight, but they were the biggest she could find in her parent's old chest of drawers. The gray sweatpants were stretched beyond whatever the material was rated for and every detail of his junk was visible. They were too short by a foot and a half, looking more like clam diggers than pants on him. The sleep shirt that had belonged to her mother was the largest top in the whole house. It was made to be extremely loose fitting but the pink words "Hot Mama" were misshapen as it attempted to cover his chest.

Kay covered her mouth to hide her laugh. He didn't know how ridiculous he looked. He didn't know how inappropriate the words were. She pointed down at her shoes and then to his own feet lacking covering. She was wearing the only ones that were in her car. She hadn't had time to go back to the trailer and had to endure working in shoes really only made for her second job. Strippers' footwear was often the only thing they wore all night and had to be flashy, fancy, and have impossibly high heels.

Oren ducked back out, presumably to find some shoes, though Kay doubted the Hope's Closet next door had any size eighteen or whatever gargantuan shoe Oren must wear. Kay took her now empty coffee carafe back to the coffee station. Margarete was getting a slice of pie for one of her customers nearby.

"Where have you been?"

"Oh, lay off, Margarete. I said I was sorry." Kay kept her eyes from rolling but just barely.

Margarete jutted out her hip and threw her hand on it. "Tara Kay, we've been worried sick. You could have called."

It wasn't like Margarete had some perfect attendance record. Kay covered for her all the time. It was one of the perks of working as a waitress in a small-town diner. They could be really shitty waitresses. It wasn't like customers had any other option for dining, unless you counted the Dairy Queen. Tara Kay didn't. "I was only a shitty little fifteen minutes late. Fucking leave it!"

The only person at the counter gawked at her language. The white-haired man with a short sleeved dress shirt, tie, and overalls (a look not seen anywhere but the deep south where every man was Brother this or Deacon that) tisk-tisked her. Kay hated that. He started in, "Use of foul language like that is a sign of the condition of your soul and…"

She didn't let him finish. No one got to preach at her while she worked, not at either of her jobs. "Oh, cram it in your Jesus hole, Churchie."

The man made a "humph" noise and rose to go. Margarete backhanded Kay's arm. "Tara! I'm sorry Brother Echoles," she apologized. "She's…she's just…you know…"

Bro. Echoles finished Margarete's sentence, "A heathen. That's what she is. A Godless, hell-bound heathen."

He glared at Kay as he put on his white straw hat with a black band that had been sitting upside down on the countertop. When he was in the middle of the dining room, Tara Kay called out, "Yeah, well, it's *real* Christ-like to stiff a poor waitress, *brother*."

Echoles' face was red as he turned back to them. He plunked down eight dollars without even looking at the bill. "Thanks," she said with a fake gracious grin. Pointedly he laid a business card down on top of the money. Kay could see it had an elaborate purple and gold cross on one side and a bible verse under his name and church affiliation. She smiled at him as she used a rolled-up napkin filled with plastic ware to slide the card back to him. "We'll take the money you owe for the food, but you can keep your crazy. We ain't buyin' any today."

He left it there and stormed out. All attention was drawn from him by the vision standing in the doorway. He muttered something about "what this world was coming to" and then was gone. Oren was back. He grinned at her, obviously over whatever had amazed him about the diner before. He pointed down at his feet. Kay just shook her head and laughed. His shoes were like a giant version of the ones she was wearing, pink sequined with five inch heels.

She got a menu for him before she remembered that he didn't speak English. That meant he probably couldn't read it either. It had pictures; he could point. She showed him to a table. Fitting him into a booth would have been impossible. He walked well in the feminine shoes, more gracefully than most women she knew. As if he didn't weigh anything, he nearly floated.

She pulled out the chair for him, but he ignored it in favor of kissing her. He wrapped his limbs around her waist and hoisted her up. He held her several feet off the ground, her chest pressed against his, and kissed her as if he had actually missed her for the hour they were apart. She was stunned to find that she had missed him too and allowed herself to melt into the kiss. It was wildly inappropriate for behavior in a restaurant but half a second in, Kay didn't care.

Oren kissed like it was his profession. With complete abandon and all-encompassing passion, their tongues tangled. A familiar voice broke her from her stupor. "Well, I guess that answers my first question about Mr. Mysterious."

Charly Boi must have come in with Oren, but Kay hadn't noticed. It was a testament to Oren's odd appearance and overall effect on her that she would miss Charly Boi's entrance. Charles, as only his mother called him, was gay and not in the "regular guy who likes other guys" way. Charly Boi was flaming and black, and in a town like Calum, that made him stick out like, well, like a flaming gay black guy in a small east Texas town.

Oren set her down and Tara Kay heard a woman say, "That explains where she's been. I might lose track of time if someone kissed me like that!" Kay and Charly Boi hugged. She'd always liked him. They were childhood friends. He understood about the difficulties of being different. He bought her drugs and medicines. He'd even seen her tree, something not many Calumites had.

Oren sat, crossing his legs at the knee. "Now see, the kiss said straight, but…" Charly Boi pointed with his wrist limp, pinkie out and zigzagged his pointer finger back and forth at Oren. "…all this, is screaming something else entirely. Please tell me that this magnificent creature is what I think he is, Special Kay."

He was the only one who used that nickname. It was one she picked out and wanted but nobody used it. She loved him a little bit more for it. She pushed him down into the chair opposite Oren and then took the chair between them. "Sorry, Charly Boi."

He cocked his head over to the side and smirked. "You sound mighty certain, little miss. And just how do you know where his appetite lies?" She didn't have to say anything. He already knew and was teasing her. "Ooo, honey! You are going to tell me every detail. But first we have got to do something about this look he's got going on. Outside, he wouldn't answer any of my questions."

"He doesn't speak any English." She pushed the menu over to Oren. She gestured eating and told him to pick what he wanted. She pointed to all the pictures and he nodded. "No, pick one." She held up three fingers. "Not three." She put one down. "Not two." She left one finger raised. "One. Pick one dinner that looks good." Oren seemed to understand and began to study the pictures a bit more carefully.

"Where the hell did he come from and does he have a brother? Preferably one that likes cock." Charly Boi leaned back in his chair and admired his view across the table.

"I don't know. He just showed up. He doesn't have a stitch of clothing. I found that stuff he's wearing in my house. Not the shoes. I don't know where he got those. He doesn't have any money or ID. He only speaks in a crazy language that sounds kind of Middle Eastern but sometimes the way he accents his words sounds Asian and sometimes it's almost Russian. I don't know where he's from, how he got here, nothing. Just that his name is Oren and he *really* likes to screw."

Charly Boi made a face like he was shocked and put his hand on his chest, but Kay knew he was just acting. He certainly had no ill feelings about a person getting what they needed physically from another. "I can't have him walking around like that. He's making me look vanilla! Me. I'll go see what they have that might fit him next door. What size shoes?"

Kay leaned down and took the shoe off Oren's crossed foot. It was the oddest thing she'd ever seen. No tag or print inside or out. There wasn't a stitch or seam anywhere. They seemed to be made in one piece and the material was soft like flower petals. The feel made her think of his penis, and she tossed the thought aside. "Doesn't say. Just get the biggest thing they have." She held the shoe up to Charly Boi's arm so he could get a measurement. It was longer than his forearm.

"You know what they say about big feet." He stood to go.

She slipped it on Oren and oddly thought of Cinderella. "Yes. And here they would be absolutely right." She mouthed "HUGE" to him and Charly Boi laughed.

"I'll be right back, Oren."

Oren stood and bowed slightly, saying, "DarlieeBoyee."

Charly Boi waved over his shoulder. Kay turned back to Oren as he sat. "Did you decide yet?" He pointed to an especially mouth-watering picture of a hamburger. "Hamburger with fries?" In the photo the burger was cut in half, exposing its cross section. He pointed to the outside of the burger where it was crispy and blackened and shook his head. Then he pointed to the pink center and nodded furiously. "Rare. Got it."

She turned to see if Ashley's table was ready, having completely forgotten about them for a bit, but they were gone. They were the only ones though. Everyone else sat staring at her and Oren, waiting, expecting something. Fucking small town rednecks, she thought.

She turned the order in to Marcos and ran around for a few minutes checking everyone's drink, making sure everyone's order was right. Regular waitress stuff. The whole time she moved around the room she was aware of Oren's hungry eyes on her. Everyone was watching her, but she was acutely cognizant of his stare, not theirs. She walked a little smoother, rolled her hips a little more liquidly because of it. She wanted him to watch her. She wanted him to *want* her.

"Where the hell have you been, Ms. Woods?!" The sheriff's voice startled her but not his tone. He had never liked her. He blamed her for Ashley's "fall from grace." He had tried to break them up at every turn. She, the daughter of a couple of dope heads, would never be good enough for his beloved son. He never accepted that Ashley was to blame for his own incarceration, not Kay.

Sheriff Whitney Stout was not a big man, but, like his son, made up for his size in attitude. He had a kind of "boy named Sue" complex. He talked with a big voice, way lower than it should have been. He must have wanted his boys to grow up with the same hardening experience because Whitney had named them Ashley and Jackie. He was handsome and slightly charming. He couldn't be an elected official if he wasn't. He also owned the liquor store on the county line. His store sold to minors. Every seventeen-year-old for fifty miles knew that. It was another reason for the animosity between him and Kay. She had provided the drugs that made his business less profitable.

"I hardly think being a little late to work is a matter for the law," Tara Kay quipped.

"A little late to…" Eyes were moving back and forth between Kay and the lawman like at they were watching the ball at a tennis game. "I don't think you realize the severity of the situation, Ms. Woods. You can't just disappear into the woods in the middle of the night. We had the whole force out looking for you this morning, scanning the area for your body. You were declared a missing person by Ashley. He thought you were dead."

"I spend a lot of time in the woods. I don't know why you're making such a big deal about this. I thought someone had to be missing for seventy-two hours before you could declare them a missing person anyway."

He stared at her for a minute before his face got red. "You've been missing since Sunday night!" When she just stared at him, he shouted, "It's Thursday!"

Kay was too stunned to react. Thursday? That meant she had been high for three nights and three days. That wasn't possible, was it? Oren was less conflicted. He didn't like the way the man with the gold star had yelled at her. He growled.

Whitney grabbed her arm. "You need to come down to the station and fill out some paperwork. I've got some questions for you."

Before Kay could snatch her arm away, Whitney was gone. Oren had the sheriff by the throat at arm's length four feet off the ground. Sheriff Stout struggled, trying to pry the sausage fingers from his neck. Oren roared in his face. It wasn't like a man yelling. It was as if they had a male lion in the diner. The glasses shook and the sheriff went still. Oren pulled Whitney's face close to his own and started singing. Singing, of all things!

Kay rubbed her arm where the sheriff had grabbed her. The bruising he had caused was already gone. How on earth was she healing so quickly? And how did she lose three days? What was happening to her? And why the hell was Oren singing?

Oren set Whitney down and then the sheriff did the strangest thing. He walked to the door and turned back, waved, and said, "You folks have a nice day," then he left. Oren turned in a circle where he stood, locking eyes with each person in the diner for a second or two while he sang. He stopped singing and sat back down. Whatever spell he was weaving with his song broke, and all the patrons went back to eating and planning their afternoons.

A couple orders came up and Margarete served them. The other waitress was acting just like all the customers. Like nothing had just happened. Like a green haired giant in pink stilettos hadn't just attacked their sheriff and then sang to them all in a foreign language. A few of them paid and left. Oren's burger was ready. Tara Kay served it to him, and he just stared at it. Kay had to show him how to hold it, how to eat it. He ate it but didn't seem to be enjoying it. She banged out a blob of ketchup and again, she had to show him how to eat it.

Kay took a French fry, dipped it in the ketchup and popped it in her mouth. She chewed and then promptly spit it out into a napkin. It didn't taste good. It tasted like chemicals, like poison, not like food should taste. Maybe the ketchup had gone bad. She tried one without. It was better but still so chemically artificial. She spit it out too.

"Don't order the fries today. Got it." Charly Boi stood at their table with a plastic bag in each hand. "Come on, handsome. Let's get you changed. Those clothes are not working for you. I even found some shoes that might fit."

Oren hadn't eaten any fries after seeing Kay's reaction to them and had struggled to eat even just half of the sandwich. Kay pulled the plate away from him. "You don't have to eat that if you don't like it. You won't hurt my feelings. Go with Charly Boi, and when you get back you can try my pie."

Charly Boi snorted and said something about thinking Oren had already tasted her pie enough. Kay punched his arm playfully like she had a million times. Charly Boi made a grimace and rotated his arm away from her. Had she hurt him?

Oren stood and took his shirt off. When he reached for his waistband, Charly Boi grabbed his hand to stop him. "Easy there, Oren. He's not much on modesty, is he?"

Kay laughed and shook her head as she cleared his plate. "You have no idea." Oren stared at her as he was being dragged off to the bathroom. Again, Kay felt like he had eyes only for her. In a backwoods place like this that wasn't a real accomplishment. Sure, there were some pretty girls in high school. Youth was always attractive, but women were past their primes faster around here. It might have something to do with how young most of them got married and started pumping out kids. They seemed worn out already at twenty five, haggard by thirty two.

"Excuse me, Tara Kay. Did I hear you say something about pie?" A woman who had once been her math teacher asked from a booth nearby.

"Yes ma'am. The orchard is producing again even though I neglected it for so long."

"You were away for a long time, Austin, wasn't it?" Mrs. McElhinny asked.

Kay nodded. She had gone to Austin to join the Daughters of Women, a coven of witches, who had eventually given her an ultimatum. Stop using blood magic and selling to outsiders or go home. She had tried to join another coven called SOFE, Sorcerers of the Five Elements, who better understood her earth magic, but they had disbanded after a traumatic event. It was an event that none could clearly remember but had robbed them all, including Kay, of their powers along with their memories.

"Well, I for one am glad you are back." Mrs. McElhinny smiled genuinely at her. Kay knew she probably was more glad the pies were back. The whole town likely was.

"I made a few on Sunday morning." Granted that was longer ago than she would have guessed but the pies would still be good if there were any left. She was glad she drove them into town before her big night. "I think I saw some apple back there."

Margarete spoke up. "I just served the last piece of strawberry pie and the peach cobbler was gone on the same day you brought it in. There's a few slices of apple left and four servings of blackberry cobbler."

Mrs. McElhinny ordered an apple and a few other patrons claimed everything else. Kay held back the last piece of blackberry for Oren and served the rest. She'd have to make more in the morning. She nuked them all in the microwave one by one and slung them. Some wanted ice cream and one even wanted melted cheddar on his apple slice, but most ate them plain. They *were* good. Kay wondered how Mr. Glenn had kept this place afloat without her pies for the few years she was gone.

Charly Boi came out and gave a little fanfare—"Dun-dada-dunt-da-da-dun!"—and presented his newest makeover. Oren strolled out of the little hallway that led to the restrooms. Kay nearly dropped his cobbler plate.

"How'd I do?"

Kay just gulped in reply.

Oren looked so good. So masculine. All traces of flamboyancy were removed. Well, not all traces; he still had green hair, but it had been cut. It didn't reach his shoulders anymore. Charly Boi had cut and styled it so that loosely resembled a Mohawk but had a kind of tall, but shaggy flat top effect. Brushed forward on the sides, it brought attention away from the odd hair color to his handsome facial features and made him look younger.

He had on a black T-shirt, probably triple X, that hugged his every bulge. His chest was impressively sculpted but his arms were chiseled. The sleeves strained but couldn't cover so he had pushed them up to end above his biceps. The pants fit, but only barely. Kay usually hated camo clothes, but the military cargo pants looked good on Oren. Charly Boi knew how she felt about hunting camouflage being worn as everyday fashion (it happened a lot in Calum) so they were probably the only pair he thought would fit. The shoes were black Converse, probably vintage by the look.

Charly Boi saw her eyes get to the feet. "Hope was so excited that she'd found a use for those shoes that she just gave them to me. She said she's had them in the back for at least ten years. She didn't think anyone with a size twenty-two would ever come into her store." He set the bags down in one of the empty chairs of Oren's table. "I got some extra T-shirts and a couple of stretchy cotton athletic shorts. He won't wear anything under so I'm taking back the underwear. I'm also taking the gargantuan pink heels to Hope. She expressed interest in them. I think she'll sell them on eBay for him. He'll need some more changes of clothes, but this was everything that would fit. Hope's going to look through all her stock and see what else she has."

Kay still hadn't said a word so Charly Boi gave her a one-armed side hug. "Pie's getting cold." He gave her a peck on the cheek. "I'm glad you're back. Love you, Special Kay." He picked up the pink shoes and left.

Kay barely noticed. She put the dark purple cobbler with flaky homemade crust and gooey dumplings in front of him and managed to stammer out, "B…bl…blackberry…all that's left."

Oren looked at the dessert from several angles. He didn't know how to eat something that messy. Kay realized his troubles and wondered what kind of man didn't know about forks and spoons. She fed him the first bite with his spoon. His eyes lit up, and not in the colloquial saying way. They actually lit up. They glowed for a minute and he smiled. She gave him the spoon. He tried to use it but the difference in size between his maw of a hand and the delicate plastic spoon were too much. Kay got him a serving spoon and he gulped the sweet goo pile down in three bites.

Oren snaked an arm around Kay's waist and pulled her down onto his lap. He put a finger under her chin and lifted her face so he could see her better. He lowered his mouth on to hers and as his lips skated across hers, her furnace ignited. She had to have him right then. Job and modesty be damned.

She pushed her tongue into his mouth and the slight aggression seemed to tip him over the edge. He jerked the front of her uniform, popping off three buttons and slipped his hand inside to cup her breast. He palmed the right one hard and then petted it. He moved up over it, letting the soft weight fall and then slid back down, pausing to pay attention to the nipple. He pinched and pulled it into a peak. Her left breast was being stimulated too by his forearm sliding on the outside of her uniform. She hadn't had a bra or panties in the old house or car, just her uniform and the stripper shoes, so she was commando today. When he removed his hand from her shirt and placed it on her leg she groaned against his mouth. She lost her breath when he pushed under her hem and found her nude underneath.

He fingered her in the middle of the cafe. His other hand rubbed her back and rear and then came to rest on her shoulder. He pressed her down so that she could feel his erection. She was about to come but suddenly her senses came back to her and she realized where she was. She opened her eyes and stood. She held her dress together in front, but no one was looking at them. They seemed to not have noticed anything.

Oren licked the finger that had been inside her and the thumb that had almost petted her pussy to climax. Kay grabbed his other hand and pulled him up out of the chair and down the hall into the kitchen. She yelled, "I'm on break!" and Margarete took over her duties without really making note.

Marcos looked at them for a second before going back to his work. She thought Oren might have even waved at him. Kay pulled him into the little alcove where the back entrance where she'd come in was. Her purse and Margarete's hung on the hooks on one side.

Oren backed her against the wall on the other. He pinned her there and then lifted her arms over her head and closed her hands around the coat hooks. He dropped to his knees and then sat on the ground. He rubbed up the outside of her thighs, pushing her uniform up to her waist where he held it. He lifted her weight off her feet and then she spread her legs for him. He moved her legs to rest on his shoulders and buried his face in her cunt. He gobbled her pie like it was cobbler.

She suffered her orgasm in silence, knowing so many ears were so close. Oren drank down her pleasure, lapping up every wave. When he stood, he spun her around so that she faced the wall. Her arms twisted and she readjusted them so she could help pull up her weight. With one hand around her hips and across her stomach, Oren unzipped his fly with his other. Kay heard it and then felt the broad smooth head pressed against her entrance from behind. She angled her hips and Oren plunged his cock inside her. This time she could not keep silent. She cried out with the ecstasy of him filling her so completely.

He fucked her hard and fast from behind. It was a position she wouldn't have thought would have worked this well, but it did. With every thrust the head of his cock touched some sensitive spot deep inside her, pushing her toward a quick and violent orgasm. Her face, forearms and breasts were the only things touching the wall. His pumping rubbed her aroused nipples against the rough finish of the cheap wood paneling. He bit her shoulder as he came. His sperm spurted against her cervix, triggering her own spasms.

He panted against her shoulder and gave her time to catch her breath before setting her down on less than steady feet. He pulled her hem down to cover her ass and turned her around. There was nothing to be done about the missing buttons of her dress and it gaped open at the chest. He kissed her neck and ear and whispered his first words in English, "I am for you, Sinnis Ina Ummum Zumru, Tara Kay Woods."

Kay didn't know what to say and so she said nothing. She found a safety pin in her purse and made herself presentable. She told Oren to go back to his table because she needed a minute to get redressed. She really needed time away from him. He clouded her mind. He was the most potent drug she'd ever had. She felt high when she was with him and not the easy-going good kind. It was the lose-track-of-where-you-are-what you're-doing-and-saying kind. Kay didn't like it, but she also didn't think she could live without it.

She expected every Calumite to be staring at her when she came back into the dining room. They weren't. Some were gone. The rest were acting as if they hadn't seen her get groped and finger-fucked and then heard her come twice in the kitchen so close to where their food was prepared.

It was a fact that what went up had to come down. She had no panties to serve as her last line of defense, and she kept expecting to have to run to the bathroom to deal with the remnants of their sex. She didn't. It was like her body totally absorbed every drop of evidence.

The rest of the afternoon went by pretty uneventfully. After all, she was just a waitress in a small-town restaurant.

THREE

Sheriff Whitney Stout hung his hat on the hat rack just inside the door of his office. There were three hanging beside it. The office was quiet as usual. The sheriff was the law in this area; there were no police, just the county sheriff and his twelve deputies. It had been a state trooper that pulled his son over those years ago. Damn troopers were always putting their noses where they didn't belong. If it had been him or one of his, Whitney could have contained the damage, but as it was the state, they had wanted to make an example of Ashley.

He could hear Ashley and his crew talking in his office. He walked past an officer doing paperwork and exchanged a head bob but nothing more by way of greeting. Whitney got a mug of coffee and went into his office. "Boys," he said as he took his place behind his desk. His office chair was leather and squeaked a little when he sat and then scooted forward.

There were three messages on the yellow paper dispatch used, laying on his desk. He glanced at them. They all said the same thing. Over the last few weeks more than two dozen people had called in to report seeing a pack of some kind of giant animals running around at night between the hours of 1 a.m. and 3 a.m. They looked like wolves but were the size of bears. There shouldn't be bears in this area. And bears did *not* run in packs, not ever. He was beginning to think the senior class had gotten together for a prank. The hours suggested it, as no law-abiding adult was up at that hour and there hadn't been any injuries. He tucked them away in the appropriate file to look at later.

"Well?" Ashley asked impatiently.

"Well, what?"

Will almost came out of his seat. "Well, what!? Where the hell has she been? What excuse did she have?"

Sheriff entered his username and password on the computer. He left it running all the time. Goddamn hippies would never convince him of human-induced global warming, no matter how many scientists they got to lie for them. "Who?"

The boys looked at each other. Jackie's eyebrows pinched together as he spoke. "Tara. Dad, we're asking about Tara Kay."

"Oh, she's fine. I'll have to cancel that missing person's report. She over at the diner working." He leafed through the files on his desk until he found hers. He wrote some notes and then closed it. The boys stared at him as he took out his sheriff's stamp and marked the front of the manila folder. It was the county sheriff emblem around a circle with crosshairs. His initials went in the top left quadrant to signal the case was closed. Double checking on his desk calendar, he added the date in the lower right.

"Dad! There's something not right about her," Jackie practically yelled.

"And she's not supposed to be with someone else…with green hair." It didn't make sense, but Ashley had tacked on the green hair bit because he knew his dad didn't want him and Tara Kay together. He didn't mention that the man scared the shit out of him. He'd never forget what happened in the woods that night. Sheriff looked at his son through slitted eyes.

Deputy Rayney rapped on the open door with his knuckles and spoke at the same time. "Sheriff, someone's here to see you." He was just a few years older than Ashley, but he was a constant reminder that the sheriff's son had done nothing with his life. Whitney tried not to take it out on his young deputy. "A suit. And he's packing. I.D. says he's from the capital," Rayney whispered, leaning his head in a bit.

Whitney knew he meant Austin, not D.C. That was the only authority folks in these parts recognized. "Secede" wasn't a rare response to the evening news; it was an everyday supper conversation. He shooed the boys up out of their seats and toward the door. "Show him in. They're just leaving."

"But we're not through," Will protested.

Whitney surveyed the one to contradict him. Ashley had always been the visible leader of the group, but the sheriff had long wondered if it was the other who pulled the strings behind the scenes. Will was smart, much smarter than his boys, and the Cunninghams were one of the first families to settle in Calum. They were used to running things. He locked eyes with Will. "Oh. Yes. We. Are." He accented every word and then added, "You leave that girl alone. She's trash and trash attracts varmints. You'll get bit every time you get involved with her shit."

THE PARKING lot was almost empty when Tara Kay pulled her old Chevette in. The car was old and had one front side panel in the wrong color, but it was hers and she loved it. She went around back to the employee parking lot. Bare A$$ets wasn't the only strip club on the county line but it was one of the oldest and most successful. And yes, they spelled it with dollar signs. They never claimed they were cla$$y.

She really didn't want to be here. Strip clubs were so pathetic in the light of day. Only the most desperate were there before the sun set, but Kay thought they were better than the group that would surely follow in the cover of darkness. Tara Kay was there for the same reason as everyone else during the day—desperation. She needed a shower, and her place didn't have running water. She parked next to a couple of very nice cars and went to the employee entrance.

Kay both wanted Oren to be there and was embarrassed for him to see her at her second job. Not many men would stick around after seeing her act. Oren had refused to get into the car when she offered him a ride, and she couldn't decide if she was relieved or upset. He had indicated that he would follow but she didn't know how. Then again, he had shown up at the restaurant remarkably fast after she left him standing in her driveway, so he must have a means of travel.

She used her key to get in. Aunt Melody accosted her before the door had time to shut behind Kay. The hug was extra tight. Melody wasn't really her aunt. There was no relation at all, as far as Kay knew. Melody had moved into town shortly after Kay's parents had been incarcerated. Kay had been a teenager but Melody treated her as if she were an adult. On the other hand, Melody had always been overly protective of Kay, disapproving of Ash from the get-go.

"Thank goodness you're all right." Melody backed up and looked at Kay. Kay dropped her eyes and walked around Melody. "You seem different." She took a couple of sniffs. "Smell different too."

Kay threw her bag on the chair at her station. A couple of lipsticks fell over and rolled onto the ground. She ignored them. "I know. I need a shower big time." She grabbed a towel off of the shelf and went into the shower stall.

"No. You smell...good. You look good too." Melody shouted over the sound of the shower starting. "You look like you spent the last few days in a swanky spa getting pampered."

"I wish," Kay yelled back. She threw her diner uniform over the door and got into the stream of water. She wet her hair first. It felt so good. She closed her eyes and just experienced. The pressure was great here, making a shower almost as good as a massage. She let it pound the muscles of her back, especially right between her shoulder blades. As the drops rolled down her body, she got the sensation that ...

"Well?"

Kay opened her eyes. "Well, what?"

"I said, where the hell have you been, then?"

"Oh, I met somebody, and we went camping for a few days." It was the best story she could come up with. She planned to tell the sheriff the same thing if he ever came asking again. She was still wondering what Oren had done to Sheriff Stout.

"You shouldn't just disappear like that, you know. You had your friends worried sick."

"I don't have any fucking friends. You damn well know that."

Melody snorted. "It's that mouth of yours! And you do too. You have me. You have Charly Boi. You should call him. He's really worried. He came here looking for you."

That alone told Kay how very worried he had been. Charly Boi wasn't just not attracted to girls. He thought girl parts were disgusting. He often told them that he preferred to think of them smooth down there, like a Barbie. That illusion was hard to maintain in here where all their a$$ets were bare.

"I saw him earlier." Tara Kay cut her shower short. She still felt high though she didn't know how that was possible. According to the sheriff she had dropped and rolled over eighty hours ago. She toweled off her hair first and then did a once over her body. She refused to think about how she could feel every thread of the rough towel or how she knew the exact brand of detergent that was used to clean them. She couldn't smell that. She was just high.

She went to her station and tugged on a matching thong and bra set. She plopped down in the chair and proceeded to dry her hair. The warmth blowing from the dryer was seductive. She only dried it partially. It suffered enough abuse that it didn't need any extra. Tara Kay sat with her back to Melody's, but they could see each other in their respective mirrors. Melody turned to look at Kay's back while the late comer finished her hair.

"Your hair looks really green. Not a root to be seen. Did you just dye it?" It was a rhetorical question. It wasn't like the hair got green on its own. "You are going to have to give up on that coloring eventually, you know." Melody was blond naturally but forced the issue with chemicals so often that her hair reminded Kay of a dandelion. Kay's hair was naturally dark, and she had to abuse her own to keep it green, so she didn't say anything about Melody's.

"Never. I'll die a green head," Kay flippantly replied. Melody wasn't listening. She was staring at Kay's back. Her tattoo had enthralled the other woman who was intimately acquainted with the ink. Kay angled her head and raised her eyebrows. "My eyes are up here."

"What? Oh, sorry. I was just daydreaming." Kay didn't believe her. Melody was still looking at her tattoo. "Can I do your eyes tonight?"

Kay shrugged. She didn't really enjoy putting on her war paint as other women did. Sometimes Aunt Melody liked to do it. She turned her chair around and Melody slid over to her. Melody stared at her for a long moment before starting in with the eye shadow. Kay thought she detected a little shake in the woman's application hand.

Melody's voice was barely over a whisper when she asked, "Do you even know what has happened? What this means?"

"What?" Kay asked without opening her eyes. She didn't want to smear Melody's work even if she was being weird.

"Nothing. Sorry. I took something crazy last night and it's making me think and say strange things. Ignore me." The liner and mascara were applied without another word.

Something about Melody's smell reminded Kay of Oren, but she couldn't put her finger on it. Her perfume wasn't changed. Melody's body smelled vaguely of Kay's new lover. Kay's mouth started to water as she saw her "aunt" in a whole new light. Something about the woman drew Kay to her. She *wanted* Melody.

"There. All done. You look perfect." Melody made a slight bow to Kay as she backed up.

Kay heard her music and barely had time to get her outfit on before her cue. She didn't look at the mirror. She walked onto the dark stage. She shouldn't have been able to hear Melody back in the dressing room over the music, but she did. She heard Melody say into her cell, "I swear. He is risen. He lives. And he has taken his Sinnis. Our queen is my ward. An earth witch."

CHARLY BOI loved his car. It had started out as an old Buick, but he had totally customized it to his tastes. The inside was ultra lush with extra cushy seats, covered in zebra print with lime green stitching. It was old enough that it had bench seats even in front, and Charly Boi drove with his right arm resting on the seat's back. The dashboard and interior of the doors were maroon at one time but had faded to a pink that went well with the rest of the car. Carpets were all redone in lime green.

The paint was his favorite color—lime green. The top was what he called "pimp topped." It was the same color as the bottom, but it had gold flecks embedded in the paint that made it sparkle in the sun like diamonds. No one else had anything like it. All the chrome work on the outside was custom too. The front grille said "Charly Boi" as did the rims. They were modified spinners that showed his name only when the wheels were moving.

He might live in a hovel, but no one knew it from seeing him about town. He presented himself as a man of means and no one, save Tara Kay, had ever seen his home. There were no apartments in Calum. He came by his home the same way everyone else here did. Inheritance. Charly Boi was at least twelfth generation Calum, but family records were hazy at best. His family had been there as long as the Cunninghams and Stouts, only his had been slaves.

His car was his life. So when he hit an animal with it on the highway that night, his first thought was that his car was ruined, not that he might die. A squirrel or even a raccoon or opossum he would have passed over with no damage, but this was no 'coon. Charly Boi hit a furry brick wall.

The creature was unlike anything he had ever seen but it was dark and, in a wreck, no one is at their most attentive. It could have been a giant wolf or maybe a bear walking on all fours. His bumper and grille area smashed into its broad side, stopping the car's forward motion instantly.

Charly Boi sat for a second catching his breath and totaling up the cost of body work he was going to have to have done to get his ride back the way he liked it. He was about to take his buckle off and get out of the car. He needed to get away from the wreckage to be safe in case somebody came over the hill behind him. A giant clawed paw smashed into the hood.

The animal was still alive. It used the hood to pull itself up. The noise was so loud, the five-inch claws scraping and poking through the metal, the metal groaning. Then the head came into view and all thoughts of his car's condition fled. Charly Boi felt sure he was going to die. There was no way he was going to survive if this animal decided to attack. His car was a lover, not a fighter, built for beauty not strength.

The animal was all muzzle and teeth. Its eyes glowed red in the dark. Its face was illuminated for an instant as the semi-trailer truck came over the hill and smashed into the tail end of Charly Boi's car. It pushed the car and the creature forward at an angle, off the road. The creature roared but the sound cut off with its head. It was crushed between the front of the car and a giant old tree. It was decapitated and the newly freed head smashed into the windshield with a red splat, causing Charly Boi to scream. It rolled off and landed somewhere outside his door.

When he quit screaming, Charly Boi dialed 911, thankful he had reception. He told the calm lady on the other end what had happened, including a description of the animal. She said that they had a lot of calls about those. He thought she even sounded a little pleased that they would now have a dead one to examine and determine what it was. She did not, in his opinion, express the proper amount of sympathy about the loss of his car.

He had just hung up when his driver's side door was torn from its hinges. He could see it sliding away from him on the highway, sparks kicking up from its contact with the road. What could rip a car door off, he wondered in that frozen moment. Then there were more glowing eyes, multicolored this time, and singing.

Everything else melted away.

∞

TARA KAY'S old beat up Chevette slid to a stop in front of the stone house she had lived in with her parents. Papaw gave it to them when he had grown too old to take care of all the land and cattle. They had let it fall into ruin. It was condemned after the cops who hauled Kay's parents off to jail saw the condition it was in.

Papaw had built it for his new wife after the war. Mamaw had married him after only having known him for two weeks. She always said that was how love was. Sometimes you just know. He had built the frame with lumber and the occasional sapling thrown in when he ran out of money. For a while there was no Sheetrock, just cardboard interior walls. The exterior walls were what really made the house special. The whole thing was bricked in local rock that Papaw had plowed out of the acreage he planned to use as his vegetable farm.

Tara Kay loved that house. It looked like it belonged there, made from the earth as it was. She blew past it without a thought this time though. She ran as fast as her legs would move, her only thought was for her tree.

Melody had put her in a panic. She'd said that they were really worried when they saw that her tree was gone. There hadn't been any reports of one, but it looked like a twister had yanked it out of the ground. Knowing how she felt about her tree, Melody had feared that Kay had done herself harm after seeing its destruction.

Melody was surprised when Kay had bolted. The girl had no idea that anything odd had befallen her beloved tree. She must have been preoccupied indeed to have gone so many days without checking on it. Their boss, Crash, had yelled at her but Kay didn't hear him. She left in the middle of her shift. She grabbed a baby tee from the backseat but that was all she had time to add before the drive. She ran through the woods now in just her stripper thong and that tiny shirt. Choosing to go barefoot, she'd tossed the ridiculous sparkling heels into the back.

Tara Kay crumpled onto the ground at the place where her tree once stood. She choked back a sob as she gazed onto the blank spot that so accurately reflected how she felt. The roots were still there but the tree was gone. It looked violent and ragged. Her heart hurt. Oren knelt behind her, wrapping his arms around her. She fought and screamed at her loss, and Oren let her. He took her thrashing and, when she was done, he wiped her tears with the pad of his thumb.

"*Ammeni baku?*" he asked.

Kay gestured. "My tree. My fucking tree is fucking gone! Gone! Destroyed while I was on a bender. With you!" She howled her words.

Oren rocked her. "*Darisam baltu oren.*"

Tired of dealing with his lack of understanding, she pushed away from him. She was angry and wanted to be alone. She stood with her toe pressed against a root. The root she had busted her lip on that fateful night. She watched as a tear splashed on the dark copper brownish-red reminder of her last night with her tree.

Oren stepped in front of her, standing in the freshly turned soil and root bits. "*Darisam baltu oren.*"

It was as if he was disrespecting a grave, and not just any grave but the one of her closest friend and relative. "I know your fucking name is Oren. Get out of there!" she yelled. She shook her head trying to clear her vision. She couldn't believe what she saw. The lower half of Oren had changed. His feet and legs grew out of the root system. His skin thickened and roughened into bark. His fingers lengthened and twisted into branches. Each strand of hair thickened and flattened into leaves.

Too overcome to think, Kay touched the familiar texture of the thick bark. She studied every detail and none came up wanting. Oren *was* her tree. If that part of her clouded drugged night was real, then what else about that night was real? Flying? Drinking blood? Being buried alive?

She climbed up as she had a thousand times and nestled into her favorite crook, which was still worn smooth from her many hours of resting there over the years. His face appeared like that of a forest fairy or tree elf, and she wondered why she'd never noticed it before.

"*Darisam baltu oren,*" it said.

Kay wished she could understand him.

"He says that he's the forever living tree." Tara Kay almost fell from her perch at the new voice. She peered out at the man from who it'd come and almost lost her balance again. The man was gorgeous. Native American, his caramel skin and blue-black silken hair matched his smooth velvety tenor voice. His teeth flashed white in the moonlight. "Aren't you a little old for tree climbing?"

Tara Kay tried to think of a witty come back. "Aren't you a little…" Nothing came. "Who the fuck are you anyway, to be judging me?"

The smile slid from his face and he dropped to one knee. "You are right. Forgive me, Sinnis Sarrum. Allow me to introduce myself. I am Hurrit, child of light, born of Sarrum Arakiel Maru, surrogate guardian of his family line."

"Well, Hurrit, you're trespassing on my family land, so if you don't want me to call the sheriff, you'll answer my questions. Why are you here? What do you want? And, since you know that crazy language Oren speaks: what the fuck is Sinnis? He keeps saying that like it should mean something to me."

There was that smile again. He angled his head to try and see through the foliage to her. "The answer to all three are the same: you, my queen."

MONTANA WATCHED from a mile away. It was as close as he would get without knowing what he was up against. He still wasn't sure after seeing it with his own eyes. The giant was obviously a Nephilim, but he was unsure about the girl. He didn't want to have a run-in with another of whatever that female warrior was back in Austin. He rotated his left shoulder. That woman had mopped the floor with him and his men like they were green recruits instead of the war hardened soldiers that they were, when they invaded her coven's compound. She had smashed his shoulder with a punch. A woman had taken him out of commission with her fist.

He remembered his words to Brian. "She didn't just dislocate my shoulder. She broke my clavicle in three places, tore, not stretched, not pulled, but ripped, no, *destroyed* every ligament and tendon holding my arm to my body. She turned my muscles and cartilage into jelly a full five inches out from her strike. Hell, she hit me from the front and somehow managed to pulverize my shoulder blade. She was a trained warrior, much more skilled at combat than her male partner, and though she didn't have wings, she glowed like them. She moved like them. And when we finally managed to shoot her with the tranq, she fell like them. She had no weapons. She caused enough damage with just her fists and feet. With all the hurt she put on us, she could have easily snapped our necks or morphed her arm into a sword like they usually do. She could have cut us in two. Hell, she could have torn us in two. It was almost like she was restraining herself. I don't know what the hell she was, but I hope they never make another like her." He had warned his leader about the woman, but they had no idea what to make of her. She had later taken out his whole unit and their base while Montana was away recovering from his shoulder replacement surgery.

She had been looking for something that Montana had. He hadn't even told Brian about retrieving it from their compound. The DakuAhu was a dagger of untold power. It was the only thing that could kill the Nephilim and Akhkharu in a way that they couldn't regenerate. Montana had kept it safe, kept it hidden all through recovery and rehabilitation. He'd tested it on a human and discovered absolutely nothing. The human hadn't died from a single slice as the Nephilim were said to, but he couldn't be sure if it was supposed to work that way on humans. Nephilim were halfbreeds so who knows what alien part of them it worked on.

He had done his research and it made him wish for Brian. Brian had always been the one to find secrets no one else could. Montana was a leader of troops; Brian was in research and development. That man knew his way around a library and laboratory. Had known, at least. The same female who'd hurt Montana had killed Brian. Montana had a harder time with anything that wasn't combat. The Paion had offered access to all of their records once they heard that a female Nephilim had come into existence and destroyed one of their cells. They wanted her dead quickly before any more of her kind were made. She was the first recorded female, and she marked the beginning of the end. Her kind would grow in number and power. She and her two "sisters" would take over this world.

Montana wasn't sure how much of the prophesies he believed in. Sure, there were things in this world that were supernatural, but the rantings of ancient women were a little too steeped in superstition and religion for his tastes. He had only found a little out about the DakuAhu because it was linked to a woman named Ereshkigal who kept coming up in his research. He had been careful not to request much information on the weapon that didn't have Ereshkigal as its main subject. He didn't want anyone, especially the Paion who could take it from him, to know he had possession of such a thing.

In the end, it wasn't the research that had revealed its secrets. The DakuAhu spoke to him for the first time after cutting that man. He was just a random man who had angered Montana. He wasn't what the dagger thirsted for. The message became clearer with every coat of blood. It wanted the life of witches. It wanted him here in this horrible little town. It wanted Montana to open a window, a portal. It wanted Nephilim and Akhkharu blood alike.

Even with it on him at all times, he couldn't work up the courage to confront a Nephilim. He didn't feel ashamed about that either. He had survived some of the nastiest battles of this generation during his duty with the military. He had faced death more times than he could remember. It wasn't cowardice; he knew what they could do. If that girl down there with the talking tree was like the woman in Austin, she could easily kill him with barely a thought.

The DakuAhu wanted her blood.

Montana backed away silently, never taking his focus off of her through his night vision binoculars. He was only a mile away. He could attract their attention from here with a wrong step. He needed to talk to those three boys again. They would be his connection to the girl and possibly his distraction. They would let him get close enough to feed the DakuAhu.

THE WOMAN at dispatch practically jumped on him as soon as Sheriff Stout sat down at his desk. She never did that. He frowned at her. She knew better.

"Was it a bear?" she asked, her eyes wide.

"No, just a deer." He flipped on his computer monitor.

"It didn't sound like a deer caused that wreck. It was a bear or giant wolf. Just like all the other calls." He just looked blankly at her. She pointed to his desk. "Two more came in while you were out."

He waived her out. "This wasn't related to the bear pack sightings. It was just a deer. Saw it myself."

"They're not just sightings anymore. Ol' Jameson lost two head 'a cattle. They's chewed up, insides all eaten. His place is close to the accident sight, ain't it? Out there by the highway?" She tried to help him see how what he was saying didn't make any sense.

He just stood and walked past her. "Better go see about Jameson," he said as he took his hat back off the peg. Jameson was a major contributor to his last campaign and expected a certain amount of preferential treatment from the sheriff he helped elect.

THE TRAILER was closer to the tree site, but Tara Kay didn't really want to take Hurrit or Oren there. She wasn't positive Oren would fit through the door anyway. After changing from tree form back to what she considered his normal look, Oren was nude. Hurrit either didn't notice the nudity or he had no problem with it. Even so, she was under dressed for company. While the two men talked quietly in a foreign language, she grabbed a pair of jeans and a bucket of ice from the trailer. She led the way back toward the stone house.

It wasn't really in any shape for company either, but she only had two places to choose from. The trailer was out because of size, so the stone house was her only choice. It had no running water or electricity, but she had some sun tea in jars on the porch. She could at least offer everyone some iced tea when they got there.

As they approached the house, Kay stopped and stared in open-mouthed abandon. The roof was solid again, covered not with shingles but thatched, and the collapsed right side was repaired. The house had not looked this sturdy since, well never. It looked better now than it did in the pictures of Papaw and Mamaw when they were just Dean and Cathleen.

Hurrit's caramel voice eased her out of her shock. "Sarrum Arakiel repaired it while you worked tonight. He knows how much it means to you and wanted to give you something. A gift as thanks for waking him from his slumber and accepting him under what must be hard to comprehend circumstances."

She knew he meant Oren even though he called him Sarrum Arakiel. So that was his name. So odd. When she turned to talk to Hurrit, she caught him staring at her neck. She didn't make anything of it, after all she was quite used to men staring at her breasts when they thought she wasn't looking, but Hurrit seemed embarrassed. He also seemed unwilling or unable to tear his gaze away from her pulse. "How did Sarrum do it so quickly? And all alone?"

"Sarrum Arakiel accomplished this so quickly with the help of his magic and his mother earth's aid." A sound of displeasure from behind him prompted Hurrit to say, "He wants you to continue using the name you gave him. It pleases him."

"But what's his real name?"

"The true name of a Nephilim is their most highly guarded secret. I only know him by his title and surname. He is Sarrum Arakiel Maru to me and all his children. That means King, son of Arakiel."

Tara Kay might be a pagan, but she had grown up in the bible belt. She knew what a Nephilim was. "So Oren is king, bred from a human women and a fallen angel named Arakiel, who has magical powers in addition to being able to turn himself into a tree AND he has kids of his own. Fucking hell."

Hurrit smiled at her and she felt a little lost in his liquid obsidian eyes. "Yes. And no. I will explain everything as he wants you to understand it." Staring at her, his face lost its smile and his eyes went back to her throat. He looked thirsty.

Tara Kay had been so long without house guests that she'd forgotten her manners. "Of course. Come in and make yourself at home. I'll pour us some tea if you'll bring it in off the porch for me."

Oren grabbed the jar and opened the door for her. Hurrit answered before she had time to ask, "He understands every word you say. He will be able to speak English soon enough. He could speak haltingly now but he doesn't wish to speak until he is sure he won't sound ignorant."

Kay barely heard him. She was staring at the living room of her childhood home. The wooden floor had long ago rotted out and it had been dirt as long as Tara Kay could remember. Hard packed from years of use, it had been clean, or as clean as dirt could be, but now it was covered in low pile emerald-green carpet. She slapped the ice bucket into Hurrit's stomach and then dropped down to all fours.

She crawled into the house, running her hands along the ultra-soft floor covering. Hurrit's gaze must have wandered in a way that displeased Oren because the Nephilim growled at his child. Hurrit walked around her and into the kitchen carrying both the ice and the tea. Kay looked closely at the new green feature of her family room. It wasn't carpet. It was moss. Thick, soft, cool unnatural moss grew inside her house.

Oren sat in a bean bag chair that barely made a sound. It looked more like a puffball mushroom. He gestured that Tara Kay come to him. She did and he lifted her into his lap. She should be sleepy and tired after a full day of work, but she wasn't. Not really. It did feel good to relax into Oren's embrace. He kissed the top of her head and tucked her below his chin. "For you, Sinnis TeRAkay," he whispered in English.

She could hear Hurrit in the kitchen. Clinking glasses and ice told her that he was doing what she had planned, serving iced tea. She took the time to look around at the other work Oren had done. All the walls were stripped away so that the stones were visible from the inside too. Interior walls were now made of stone too, thought they were newer and very smooth. The old moldy furniture and decrepit remnants of her childhood had been removed. Shelf mushrooms formed floating shelves where some remaining knickknacks sat. The place was clean and bright.

It was then that she noticed the light. The house had no electricity, having been cut after Kay's parents couldn't or wouldn't pay the bill. The lines weren't really safe anyway, having been installed by Papaw in the sixties. They ran on the outside of the walls, not hidden inside as would have been up to code. They were gone now, removed with everything else, but still the room was filled with light. A normal enough looking lamp stood on either side of every seat and an ornate yet organic looking chandelier hung from the center of the room. They didn't so much shine as they did glow. More mushrooms; had to be. It was a trippy world she lived in now.

Hurrit called from the other room, "Your earth witch abilities far exceed any I have seen. This house is amazing. I wonder if you might be willing to come to my home and do a little 'remodeling.'"

"I didn't do this. My grandfather built this house. Sixty years ago! It's been condemned since I was fourteen. It was one step above rubble this morning. Oren must have done it." So this was what he'd been up to while she was stripping. This was what he insisted on staying for. It only took him a few hours too. "How?"

"His magic works in much the same way yours does, I imagine. He speaks to the mother, communicating through his blood, and she answers with gifts of what he needs." Hurrit came in with three jars of tea. He didn't know that her abilities were gone. They all three sat sipping tea. It was tasty, not as disgusting as the soda she'd tried to drink at the club, but it did nothing to quench her thirst, and from the look on Hurrit's face, it did nothing for his either. Tara Kay broke the uncomfortable silence. "So I'm a Sinnis. What's it mean?"

Oren spoke quickly to Hurrit and the man nodded his head. Kay didn't give the man time to interpret. "What language is that? Where are you guys from?"

Hurrit set his now empty glass jar on the toadstool beside his puffball "chair." "Sumerian. And we are not from the same place. Or time. Sarrum Arakiel was born in ancient Mesopotamia, what would become Sumer, before it could even be called a civilization. He was born over nine thousand years ago, though time was counted less universally than it is now, so his exact age is impossible to know. He came to me in a spirit walk when I was a young adult. I had a wife and a son when he made me vitala, who were both dead from old age by the time he left me as protector of his family line while he slept. I am now over six thousand years now myself."

Kay tried not to freak out about the numbers that were being thrown around so casually. She needed to call the Daughters of Women and tell them about this. They needed to know, but she was still mad at their Abbess, Nathalia, for throwing her out. If she was honest with herself, she knew that Nathalia hadn't thrown her out, but had given her a choice. Kay had chosen wrong and almost got herself killed in a SOFE circle. She knew it was true as soon as she thought about it, but she couldn't recall any details of what happened to her.

"You were human, but he made you vitala. What's that? And how did he 'make' you into anything?"

"You would know it by the more modern name: vampire. I live on blood but need very little to survive. In fact, that is how he chose me to be his surrogate guardian. He held a competition to see who among my tribe could deny themselves the longest in the face of great temptation. I went for one hundred four days without food or anything to drink other than water. All the while a huge feast was held around me and the other seven contenders, my brothers. We had to fulfill our normal duties with no nourishment. I beat them all. Vitala are made in exactly the way folklore says vampires are made." He paused. "Sarrum Arakiel's blood is very powerful. He chose to give it to me and in exchange, I protected his family line to ensure you were born. I am his oldest child."

"You said you were his child of light, but in every story I know of, vampires are not real fond of sunlight."

Oren spoke to Hurrit again for an extended period and when he had finished, Hurrit started again. "Sarrum Arakiel is the first Nephilim born. Nephilim live on the prana, or life force, found in every living thing, always battling the hunger inside them. If they give into their hunger beast and take another Nephilim's blood, they become Akhkharu. Akhkharu are violent and evil. Their bodies cannot stand the light of the sun and their blood creates children of darkness. Their creations are the opposite of the Nephilim. The Nephilim struggle against the hunger that could destroy them until the time of the Sinnis. The prana of their Sinnis will quench their thirst. Sinnis means woman. Your full title is 'Sinnis Ina Ummum Zumru'. You are the woman from his mother's body. You are destined for each other. Your blood has already quenched his thirst and tamed his beast. He will serve you for all eternity."

FOUR

Abbess Maeve Lovejoy watched from the window as her daughter, Genevieve, toddled across the yard. Genevieve was a beautiful child. She'd been born with a head full of dark hair to match Maeve's. The Abbess, whose rule was almost exactly as old as her daughter, had worried when a few months later all that chocolate brown hair had fallen out. It was quickly replaced with golden red. Aaron, Maeve's mate, assured her that his did the same thing when he was little.

Genevieve was petite; Aaron and Maeve weren't tall, but they also weren't terribly short either. She was absolutely dwarfed by the guardian who followed her toddling closely. Harrith Samsiel Maru was "He who is for the One," and he was convinced that Genevieve was that promised messiah. Maeve wasn't sure. Every parent thought their daughter was a princess, but a goddess was a little harder to believe. Sam, which was what Maeve and everyone else had taken to calling him, had barely left the baby's side since her birth. Maeve didn't think that a single injury had befallen her little one in all those first days of learning to walk. Her diapered and padded rump had never felt the thud of failure. Even now Sam walked on his knees behind her, giving aid almost before it was needed whenever Genevieve teetered. They were going to have to invent a new word—spoiled didn't nearly cover it.

Sam had given Maeve his true name. This was apparently a mark of great honor and trust with the Nephilim. She knew she could use it to bind him, banish him, if she needed. She would, if Genevieve was ever in any danger, but so far Sam had only ever shown her daughter acute attention and proper love. Like any new mom, Maeve worried incessantly about her child, but she had an added level of worry. If what Nathalia told her was true, she didn't just need to keep Genevieve safe for her own peace of mind but because if the child were to die it would signal the end of all mankind.

A knock on her open door broke her train of thought. She turned to see Nathalia step into the room. These had been Nathalia's quarters, both private and public, when she'd been Abbess. They were now converted into Maeve and Aaron's room, Genevieve's nursery, and Sam's room, which was really just a hallway space that was large enough for him to stand in. The man almost never slept and even more rarely left Genevieve's side.

Good Morning. Nathalia spoke, not out loud but inside Maeve's head. That was her skill; Nathalia was a Vinco, meaning she broadcasted her thoughts and feelings into other people's minds. She couldn't speak. Her vocal cords were destroyed when she cut her own throat two years ago. She had done it to sever the magical hold an ex-boyfriend had over her. He had been a SOFE, meaning Sorcerers of the Five Elements, a rival coven to the Daughters of Women, to which Maeve and Nathalia belonged. It had worked. Nathalia committed suicide and funneled her death through Michael, killing him.

"Mornin'. I know I'm running a little late. I can't tighten this corset by myself." Maeve was a tight-lacer. She wore a corset of one type or another at least seventy percent of her waking time. Today she was wearing her favorite, her first. It had been a gift from Nathalia when she was Abbess to Maeve in acknowledgment of her ascension to Vinculum Primo, the Daughter's highest rank.

Maeve wasn't just the Abbess. She was their Vinculum, their matchmaker, their bridge from the couples she made to the Holy

Capacitors who collected and stored the energy those couples made. Capacitors served as a kind of magical energy storage system from which all sisters could pull from and use. The restrictive corsets encased her heart and reminded her that her body, and her very life, was a tool, a source of power for all the sisterhood. She had a great power, extremely rare and prized by the Daughters, so she had heavy responsibilities. The corsets served as physical reminders of the restrictions her position placed on her, restrictions that Aaron and their special relationship had eased.

Nathalia crossed to where Maeve stood. Maeve gripped the window frame and Nathalia untied the strings of the corset. Wrapping the ends around her wrists, Nathalia pulled steadily. She adjusted a few threads here and there until the corset was a tight as it could be. She quickly tied it off. *You're going to need a new set soon if you don't stop losing weight. The edges of this one are now touching. I can re-lace them differently so that we can overlap them but they won't lay the way you like them. I'll have the French chapter send over some material. You still use the same corsetiere over on Lavaca?*

Before Nathalia's conversion, that much conversation broadcasted into Maeve's head would have made them both sick and weak. Nathalia was Sinnis Ina Ummum Zumru of Eiran Kafziel Maru. It meant Nathalia was the woman of the Kafziel family line and mate of Eiran. Eiran had found Nathalia in her last moments. She had been dying from the self-inflicted wound to her throat and Eiran had given her his immortal blood, forever changing her. Into what they were still unsure, but what it had done to her abilities was undeniable.

Maeve nodded. "She's semi-retired now, though. Closed shop a few months ago. She still does the work, thank goddess, but she does it from her home. I've got her contact info in my office somewhere." That's where they were headed anyway.

The office had been moved across the sanctuary to what they had used as a conference room before. It had more room, was still conveniently located, and served very well. They needed an office with more space because, though Maeve was Abbess, she and Nathalia shared the tasks of that position. Maeve kept normal business hours there and she kept her baby with her most of the time. With Genevieve came Sam and sometimes Aaron. Nathalia was needed there and with her came her Nephilim, Kafziel Maru. They were all involved with decisions that affected Daughters and Nephilim and so the much larger office was already needed even before day's petitioners came in to have audience with them.

Maeve tugged out the ivory chopsticks she used to hold her hair and her hair came tumbling down. She tossed them onto the counter by the mirror and grabbed the brush. Nathalia took it from her and ran it through the mane until it was so shinny that it reflected. Maeve's power was not linked to her hair, but it was enhanced by it. Severely straight and the darkest of brown, her thigh length locks mesmerized and entranced everyone. Though Aaron joked about how he was constantly finding them threaded through his chest hair, Maeve knew her flowing mane put everyone at ease. It relaxed, opened them up to the spells she could cast.

Maeve led the way out and across the sanctuary. She and Nathalia didn't spare a thought about the room's rare beauty. They had grown accustomed to its cavernous size, rosy Plexiglas ceiling that provided natural light, and stone inhabitants. The erotic images of women, some single, some coupled, some in small groups, appeared to be ancient carvings. They were in fact the bodies of Capacitors whose constant exposure to the collected power had petrified them.

There were already people lined up outside, waiting. They greeted Maeve cordially and casually. Getting rid of the formal greetings according to rank was one of the first things she did as Abbess. She smiled and greeted them back. She didn't have to tell them how to order themselves. They knew how the hierarchy worked. It wasn't first come first serve. Women came first, and within that was Primos followed by lower ranking Sophomores, Novices, and un-pledged. Then children and men, of which there were few that needed to stand in line. Ninety percent of children and men living on the compound were linked to Daughters who would bring their requests to the Abbess. Lastly came the Nephilim, as they believed they deserved, as halfbreeds.

Maeve and Nathalia entered a room already occupied by several Primos, and Eiran closed the door behind them. Libby, the Daughters' eldest active member, was there with her books. Jolie and her toddler, sat on the floor. Ingrid, dressed as the hippie she was, stood near a window. Camilla's tiny frame, well into her second pregnancy, was huddled on her Nephilim, Nanae's lap. Camilla was only the second claimed and converted Sinnis in the world. Nephilim were barren and their Sinnis were thought to be also, so her pregnancies were nothing short of miracles. Izzy, the third of their trio, must be in their apartment, caring for their first son.

After pleasantries were exchanged and Ingrid served her magic infused tea, Jolie gave her dream journal to Maeve. It was an unspoken agreement that Jolie should always go first. She was the groups Animaverto; she saw the future in her dreams. "I'm having that same dream again, the one where I'm in the SOFE circle. The same glowing tear in reality and feelings of euphoria followed by panic and pain. The light that seems to be shining on us, favoring us, is really being pulled from us, the ones locked in the circle. It is our power and then our life, being taken. Then something steps through the tear. I should say someone because it is definitely a person, but it's got no gender, no features, other than a general human shape. It's made of light and I know it's feeding off of my life. I die. Everyone in the circle dies. I always wake up screaming. It is horrible and if we can't figure out what it is a warning for soon…I feel like I get closer to dying every time I have the dream, and one night the shining one might actually take my life."

"But you don't recognize anyone there with you? Does the place seem familiar at all?" Libby spoke from her place on the couch. She was responsible for recording the achievements of the Daughters of this sect. She had access to the histories and had been trying to solve this with Jolie for weeks now.

Jolie shook her head no. "It's wooded around the clearing." She shrugged. "Some of the trees have spots of bright color."

It happens at the beginning of fall, then. We have some time, at least, to avert this from happening again. You're sure it isn't just a remnant of the last time? Nathalia could not only broadcast to a single person but a group of her choosing. She could speak to the whole world if she wanted.

"Definitely not. It's a different place altogether." Juliet started to whine when her mother Jolie ignored her sign for milk. She pulled at the neckline of Jolie's shirt. Jolie distracted her with a biter biscuit, but knew it wouldn't work long. It was time to nurse.

"Seems clear that it's going to happen again." Both Nephilim in the room grunted in agreement with Maeve's statement. The Nephilim knew that the Shinar would be relentless in their attempts to come through the veil into this world. The Shinar were made of life, they needed to take from other worlds to survive. Earth was of great importance to them as it had, not only abundant naturally occurring life, but a large portion of Shinar power in the shape of Nephilim. "Next time you have the dream, try to ignore the events. I know that's mostly impossible when you are in actual pain but try. Concentrate on your surroundings. If we can figure out where the gap in the veil will be, we can get a Nephilim circle there to close it."

Jolie stood, bringing Juliet with her. She took her dream journal and her baby and left without another word. This wasn't a compound where chores magically did themselves. Each woman had her share of work to do to keep this place running. It was time for Jolie to get started on hers.

"Speaking of getting a Nephilim circle together, how's Minali doing?" Maeve asked Camilla. Minali was a Siren, a breed of witch this coven had never known, who could call groups to her across oceans. She'd come from another compound in Ethiopia that had suffered greatly under the attack of an Akhkharu and his children of darkness. She had been the only survivor to make the move with her coven's Capacitors.

Camilla stood with a little help from Nanae. The move from his lap to standing actually made her shorter. Camilla was the tiniest of women and only a half inch stood between her being a little person and her being an actual "little person." Camilla shook her head and shrugged slightly. She didn't speak much. Her face said it all.

Minali wasn't doing well. Physically Camilla, the healer, could find nothing wrong. There was nothing to be fixed, yet Minali was wasting away. When she first came to them, they had hoped to use her ability to gather Nephilim. She claimed to be able to call specific groups even if she had little or no knowledge about them. Her mother had a variation of the same talent, that had not been diminished by joining the Capacitors. She could attract individuals, but only those she knew. If she wanted a person near her, the compulsion to comply was irresistible. With Minali's mother having lost everyone she knew in the attack, her compulsion was focused on Minali. Minali had to be near her mother.

Not only had Minali been unable to bring new Nephilim out of the woodworks, the ones that already resided there with the Daughters had reported that their need to stay close was fading. Minali's powers had faded slowly. When they had gone, her health had quickly followed. Minali, when she'd arrived, was a true beauty with flawlessly smooth mocha skin and long curly brown sun lightened hair. Her fine delicate facial bone structure was complimented by a striking set of large liquid black eyes and full lips. All that had worked for her, now worked against her, making her seem more sick, more off. Her skin was blotchy and pale; her hair was stringy and had started to fall out. Her delicate facial features and large eyes made her seem frail and weak.

"I have been doing some research. I went through the books on loan about Sirens and this has never happened to one. It isn't about her ability. So far I haven't found any records that match her decline in power and then health, but I'll keep looking. I know it's there somewhere." Libby wasn't going to give up. Minali had moved in with her and her husband Leonard when their son Billy had left. They had empty nest syndrome and she'd just lost everyone she'd ever known. They had bonded. Libby loved Minali like the daughter she never had, and she wasn't about to lose her. No with so much knowledge and ability at their disposal.

"She hasn't responded to any of my concoctions. Maybe if Tara Kay could come back, she could grow something tailored to Mina…"

No. Nathalia interrupted Ingrid. *Your apprentice made her choice. She chose SOFE and nearly got herself killed. The rest of us too. No, we won't be bringing blood magic back to the Daughters.*

"That isn't your call to make," Maeve said softly.

Nathalia tried to keep the fire from her eyes. *She almost got Aaron killed. You want that black magic back, infecting our flock?* She spoke only to Maeve, but Maeve didn't answer her question.

Maeve hated to argue with Nathalia. They'd been friends their whole lives and lovers for years. Nathalia was used to being in charge, but this was exactly why Maeve was Abbess now. She would lead the Daughters into their next era. Maeve never tried to interject her rulings into Nephilim politics. "If any of us can help Minali then we have to try. Even if we don't agree with Tara Kay's methods, I say we reach out to her."

"I've tried, Abbess. I left her messages, but for the past year or so her cell has been dead. I'm worried about her. I don't know any other way to contact her." Ingrid was fighting back tears.

"Izzy is from the same area. Maybe he knows another way." Maeve remembered that it was Izzy who had alerted them to the possibility that Tara Kay had been growing and dealing her special brand of medicines before she left. The two weren't friends, only acquaintances, but they certainly weren't enemies. "Maybe he knows somebody who knows how she is."

Nanae spoke and they all unconsciously leaned into the intoxicating sound. "We will ask him if he has anyone there he can ask. He does not speak fondly of that place." Nanae and Camilla were mated but their union was a trinity. Israel was every bit as much their spouse as either of them. Israel was a Lilitu, a child of the light. Nanae had converted him before Camilla.

"Tell him thanks. I know revisiting the past isn't always fun." With that, Maeve dismissed the Healers.

Nanae stood and brought Camilla up with him, much in the same way Jolie had picked up Juliet. To the human eyes in the room, the two seems to disappear, just "poof" and they were gone. Nathalia and Eiran were intimately familiar with that mode of travel. They could see as Nanae dissolved his and his Sinnis' forms. Cell by cell he had broken them down to their elements. All Nephilim could tabalu that way, moving through the earth. They knew he would rebuild them wherever he needed.

Though the women weren't exact on the details of tabalu, they were almost used to it by now. They took no note of the disappearing act. Nathalia thought about Minali's possible connection with a Nephilim. She had been the one to save Minali when the Akhkharu had attacked her coven. She had accompanied Minali and the capacitors on their flight across the Atlantic Ocean. On that plane ride, Minali had told her about the special ability in their family and how she thought she might have brought the attack on.

She had said, "I think I might have attracted him. Accidentally. A few months ago I found a man in my room. I didn't recognize him, and I should have screamed for help, but he said not to be afraid, and he was so incredibly attractive that I wasn't. We talked for hours. He wanted to know all about my family and my ability, but mostly my sex life. I told him everything, things I'd never told anyone. I even talked about the capacitors. I couldn't help myself."

Minali had gone on to tell Nathalia about the sexual experience with what Nathalia had felt sure was a Nephilim. "I wanted him. I mean really *wanted* him. And I could tell he needed something from me too. It was like he was hungry. His eye lit up like flames where his pupil had been when I asked him to kiss me. He did and it was crazy good. It felt a little like licking a battery, but it was so exciting. I'm not usually aggressive at all when it comes to guys, but something came over me. I whispered that I wasn't wearing anything under my nightgown and guided the hand that was on my thigh up, to let him feel. I let him finger me. No, I *made* him do it. I'm not sure he really wanted to, but he had such a weird look on his face. He had hold of the back of my neck and kept me looking at his face the whole time. It was so freaking sexy and when I came, he literally growled at me. He let me lay back on the bed and took his fingers out of me and then tasted them. I wanted him to have sex with me, but he wouldn't. It was fine though. I didn't feel rejected or anything because he went down on me for like an hour. After that he just laid on the bed next to me. He wouldn't touch me anymore, but he stayed when I ask him to. He seemed sad but wouldn't talk about it. I begged him to let me keep my memory of it, that it was the most amazing sexual experience I'd ever had and, in the morning when I woke up, he was gone. I could remember what happened, even though his face was a little hazy and his name was erased completely. Like a month later I got the craving to move to Austin and started to feel like there was something wrong about what we had done together that night, something gross like having sex with your brother. I'd been trying to call him to me for a while when the attack happened. I wanted to know if I had made him do it and if he was feeling guilty too. I didn't want him to feel that way since I was the one who pressured him, but he wouldn't come back. I've never had anyone be able to refuse my compulsion. I was trying a new kind of calling to any magical creature like him, thinking I could snare him in a group call. My mother and the other capacitors were helping me when the fighting started that night."

Nathalia had thought at the time of telling, that the Nephilim was sad because Minali wasn't his Sinnis and he would be alone until he found her. Now she wondered if it was something else. Was Minali a Sinnis to another? Had her Nephilim turned Akhkharu and this wasting away the effect on his Sinnis? Was that connection why her ability had faded first and now her health? It would certainly explain why there was no record of anything like this. There were only two recorded Sinnis claimed and even fewer conversions, and they all resided here on the Daughters' compound.

Nathalia signaled to Eiran that she was ready to go. She filled him in on her concerns as he tabalu'd them away. She was the only one who knew the names of each Nephilim. She was the only one who could track down the one at the beginning of Minali's bloodline. She needed quiet to consider. They dissolved and disappeared.

Unaware of Nathalia's musings, after they had gone, Ingrid asked, "What about Billy? He and Tara Kay were always pretty close."

"Last I heard from him, he was up in Missouri. He says he wants to be alone. He certainly doesn't want to talk to his mama more than a couple times a month. I told him I'd give him time, but you can call. If he's near there, I'm sure he wouldn't mind looking in on her."

If Maeve had a gavel, she'd have struck it. Half the attendees had already dismissed themselves. "Call him. If there's nothing else, I need to get started on my unscheduled for today so I can get to breakfast."

TARA KAY woke up to the sun in her eyes and a warm but empty bed. Oren had slipped out at some point. He had shared her bed again last night in every sense of the phrase. She was sore in all the right places. She could get used to this kind of treatment pretty quickly and, from what Hurrit had said in the wee hours of the morning, she had forever to do it.

Kay was now immortal.

She stretched and considered going back to sleep. She decided against it. She should be exhausted. From the position of the sun, it was only about seven. Papaw was a farmer and ranch man and had built the house accordingly. The bedrooms were on the east side and living on the west. That way you didn't need clocks nor as many lights. Residents woke with the rising of the sun and enjoyed as much of the evening light as possible in the family room. If all the chores were done, that is.

She got out of bed slowly, feeling every movement and action inside her body. Hurrit had explained what had happened to her as best he could with Oren's help. She was irrevocable changed at the base level. She couldn't even be considered human anymore. A doctor would freak at a sample of her blood. It was the same as Oren's blood. What she remembered from that first night when her tree had come to life and made love to her was all true. He had drained her nearly to the point of death and replaced her human blood with his superior Nephilim blood. It hadn't stopped there. He had done something else. Something magical that even Hurrit couldn't fully explain. Something that Oren couldn't do with anyone but her.

She picked up her baby tee and thong off the floor where Oren had thrown them. She started to put them on when she noticed the two bizarre plants growing in the corner. One was slightly larger and had what could only be described as a lid on top. It looked kind of like a Venus fly trap with a waste basket sized stem. The "lid" was flat across the top and had no matching opposing side to make the normal fly trap mouth. It was fringed with hair-like cilia. She had always been fascinated by fly traps, even as a little girl, and she couldn't help herself. She reached out and ran a finger along the silky protrusions.

The plant opened up. A slender pollen-covered stamen came out toward her and she jumped back, dropping her clothes. The room was blanketed with a pleasant smell that could only have come from the pollen. It was a fucking air freshener, Tara Kay thought. Oren had really outdone himself when he remade her home.

She felt rather than heard the woman's voice tell her it was her hamper as well. The voice, she now knew, was that of the great mother earth. Oren called her Ki. Kay knew her name was really Kiyahwe but hadn't said anything. She didn't really know how she knew, and she didn't want to sound stupid.

Kay retrieved her clothes and tossed them into the waiting mouth. It closed. Crazy. Kay wondered if there was a laundry plant in the house somewhere. As she had nothing else to wear, she touched the hamper again in the way that had caused it to open in the first place. It opened but when she looked inside, there was no way she was putting her arm in there. Her clothes were there, resting on the bottom, but they were already saturated with something. The plant was digesting her clothes.

Great. Just fucking great. Now she had nothing to put on.

Kiyahwe told her to try the other plant. This one looked like spineless thistle. Sturdy and thick, it had a seamed bulb but no flower. Shrugging, she ran her finger across it. Swaying, it began to bloom. When it was done moving, she was looking at a rainbow flower the size of a small dinner plate. It only had one continuous pedal. When she touched it, the pedal broke free and landed in her hand. As she lifted it to her face, it fell open. It wasn't a flower at all.

It was a dress.

She slipped it over her head and wasn't surprised when it fit perfectly. She went down the hall.

Hurrit was sitting in her kitchen with his back to the door. "Morning," she said as she went to the sink across from him. Like everything else in this new house, it was activated by touch. Cool clear fresh water came out with the first touch and after she'd filled a glass, the second touch stopped the flow. Oren had put a step in that ran along the cabinets when he worked on the house. It made her hit the countertop at a more reasonable level. She made a mental note to thank him. He noticed how short she was and recognized what difficulties that might make for her in everyday life. She turned, rested her elbows back on the countertop, and studied Hurrit over the top of her glass.

His head was down so that she couldn't see his face, only the top of his head. His board-straight black locks fell to either side, creating a curtain of darkness around him. She couldn't suppress a shiver. "Hurrit. Are you okay?"

Without raising his eyes, he nodded his head yes and then must have changed his mind because he changed the movement to shaking it no.

"Why won't you look at me? Or speak?"

His voice, as caramel smooth as ever, had an odd lisp. "I do not want to frighten you."

"Well, fuck-all lot of good you're doing at it. Stop acting weird and tell me what's wrong." He had said she was his queen and she wondered if she should pull rank on him.

"Such colorful language the Sinnis Sarrum uses." She knew he thought her constant use of the f-bomb was amusing. She could hear the smile in his voice. "Sarrum Arakiel is communing with Ud and Ki and asked me to wait here until you awoke. I can take you to him when you are ready." He still had the lisp, like something was in the way of his tongue making the right sounds. Something like extra-long incisors.

"Holy fuck, Hurrit. You've got your vamp face on, don't you?" She sat in the chair closest to her, across the table from him. He had told her that she was faster and stronger than him or any other creature on earth, but she still felt more comfortable with something between them. He *was* a vampire. Fears so heavily ingrained in a person by culture were not so easy to shrug off. "Look at me. Let me see."

"Are you certain?"

"Just show me. I knew a face as gorgeous as yours couldn't have spawned all those tales of scary monsters." Throughout history the vampire was portrayed as the undead. Not the rotten visage of the zombie but a living corpse just the same. She wondered briefly if zombies were real, and then the world dropped out from around her.

All she could see were his eyes. They were black from lid to lid and corner to corner, like the darkness of his pupil had leaked out and coated the iris and sclera. She felt attracted to them. The black wasn't just a color. It had depth. They pulled her in, and she found herself leaning toward him. Her progress stopped when he smiled.

If his eyes had their own magnetic pull on her, his mouth flipped her around so that her poles were reversed. She was repelled by that mouth. It was filled with razor sharp incisors. Every tooth was for piercing flesh, like on a shark. She could see that there was a second row of teeth behind the frightening first, but they were blunt. His vampire teeth came down out of his gums in front of his human teeth.

"You think my face is gorgeous?"

She sat transfixed on his mouth. She couldn't tear her eyes away from those teeth. They worked up and down as he talked, fitting together so tightly, with one slipping between the two below it. She imagined how easily he could separate a chunk of meat from its owner. This time she suppressed her shiver. She didn't want him to know she was scared.

She nodded at his question. "Yes, I did."

He closed his mouth, pressing his lips tight. "But no longer?"

With his teeth hidden, she was once again focused on his eyes. Her poles reversed again, and his magnetism pulled on her but this time the shock was gone and she kept her head. She still wanted him, wanted to be near him. She was drawn to him, but it was more like how a woman should be attracted a fine man, and not like a mosquito was attracted to a bug zapper. "Yes, still. Very much. Why the change? Why now?"

Kay hadn't known that Native Americans could blush, but apparently, they could. "This is the face of my hunger. I have not fed in twenty years, but I have gone much longer without feeding. Your nearness has awakened it, Sarrum Sinnis."

"Call me Kay or Tara Kay." She added, "But never just Tara. I hate being called 'dirt.'"

Hurrit tilted his head slightly. "But you are an earth witch. And the earth is great mother to us all. Being called terra is fitting and honorable."

She had never thought of it that way and felt slightly embarrassed. She'd always thought of its use to signify dirt or garbage. It was trashy and country and she'd never liked it. Now she wondered why it was always such a big deal. She was too good to be called by a word that meant earth?! She wished she hadn't said it. She changed the subject. "You haven't eaten in twenty years? You need…blood? And I make you hungry?"

He dipped his chin once. "Yes, but I need it less than others of my kind. Sarrum Arakiel's blood is very strong, though over the years mine has weakened and I must feed more regularly than I had to at first."

"Every twenty years is more regularly than usual? I go crazy if I don't get three square meals a day." She had a suspicion that it was like runt syndrome with the tiniest puppy in a litter. She had gone so long without a regular source of food that she overcompensated by making sure she was never hungry.

Now that she was thinking of it, she couldn't remember the last time she'd eaten. Surely it wasn't the peach yesterday morning. She was hungry but nothing really sounded that good. Hurrit's voice jolted her out of her thoughts.

"I only feed when I am going to make another like myself. I drain them before giving them my blood. In the beginning there was only me. Then Sarrum Arakiel had me make four more, one assigned to each of the elements with me as their overseer. Over time you witches grew in number and I had to make more and more children to keep up with overseeing their safety. My last child is only twenty years old. Before that it was two hundred years between feedings." He took a deep breath. "Your blood smells so like his, only better. It's somehow more. Last night I kept my hunger at bay because of the nearness of Sarrum Arakiel, but today he is not here to mask your scent. May I ask you something?"

She worried about what he might ask her for, but she nodded. "How do I smell to you?"

His face, still the mask of hunger, was so serious and insecure that Kay had to laugh. "Well, you don't stink. I can't really smell you from way over there."

She wasn't sure that she could have seen him move, it was so fast, if she hadn't been enhanced by Oren. As it was, she saw it and reacted before his movement had time to register. He rose and crossed the room. She also rose but was clumsier and knocked over her chair. She backed over it and stepped up onto the riser Oren had built. Hurrit pressed his body into her personal space, pinning her against the cabinets. He didn't touch her but there were places where the space was only a hair's breadth. She froze, not wanting to trigger his predatory response any more than she already had. She did not want to be seen as the rabbit to his fox.

Thanks to the riser, they were almost eye to eye. More like eye to mouth, but thankfully he had that nightmare inducer clamped shut. He dropped his head to the side, pulling his hair aside, exposing his neck. The move was more like a dog to his alpha than a fox to his dinner.

"You cannot smell if you do not breathe," he whispered.

She hadn't realized she was holding her breath. She let it out and leaned in to get a good whiff of his skin. The faster she told him he didn't stink, the faster she got out of this situation. As soon as she inhaled, she didn't want to get out of the situation quickly anymore.

Hurrit smelled good. Damn good. Like Oren but different. It made her hungry and horny at the same time. Unbeknownst to herself, Kay grabbed a fist full of his shirt on either side of his waist. She pulled him into her, putting her nose and mouth against his dark skin. When open-mouth smelling was no longer enough, she put her teeth and tongue on his caramel covering.

His gasp wasn't his only reaction. She felt his erection grow inside his pants and press against her thigh. He gripped the countertop on either side of her, but she felt sure he was retraining himself, not pinning her in. He pushed away from her only enough to keep from crushing her as she wrapped one arm around his waist and pulled him tighter. Her other hand slid up his side, in over his chest, shoulder and up to his face. She kissed and nipped up his neck to his ear.

"You smell amazing. And you taste even better." She whispered in a way she knew would tickle and tease the sensitive skin right below and behind the ear. Her voice was throatier than she would have liked. She wondered what his blood would taste like and wasn't repulsed by the thought at all. She found herself considering what it would feel like if he bit her, and not in the fearful way she had just a few minutes ago.

She pressed his face against her neck so that they mirrored each other's position. He obligingly kissed her neck, but once he was there the kiss became more passionate than obligatory. She was painfully aware that he was careful not to let his teeth touch her skin. She wanted him to bite her, and she said so softly. She was so caught up in the sensations of the vitala pressed against her that she didn't feel her own incisors lengthen.

When she put her teeth on him, where her flat omnivore teeth would have just scraped, her carnivore teeth sliced right through. A line of blood welled up and she couldn't help but taste it. Without thinking, she opened wide and clamped down, piercing his neck in two places. His blood was delicious as it pumped into her mouth. She took three draws from it before she could pull away. The punctures healed up almost instantly, slightly faster than her teeth going back to normal.

She shrugged mentally. This was the way of it now. She continued to nuzzle his neck. "Take what you need, Hurrit. I want this," she said against his scrumptious skin. His name came out of her blood-drunk mouth as a purr.

He made a guttural noise, and an audible crack and crumble made her eyes snap open. She must have released her hold on him because as soon as he could, he stepped back. She felt the loss of him immediately and held her arms out to him. "It's okay, Hurrit. I understand the hunger and I'll heal, right?"

He shook his head no, keeping his eyes down. His breathing was ragged, and he swallowed a few times before speaking. "Feeding you is one thing but taking blood from my queen is quite another."

"Are you afraid of what Oren will say? I want this. He doesn't own me." She wished it wasn't so begging, the way her voice sounded.

He clutched his fists, hanging down at his sides. Little pebbles fell from them to bounce onto the floor. Marble pebbles. Her countertop. Again, he shook his head no, but this time he held up his hand. "Please stop telling me that you want this." He took a few more deep breaths. "I want to, but I won't until the time when you understand the true value of what you offer. It is not a thing to be given lightly. You don't know the power of your blood. Or what it will do to you to give that to me." He seemed more in control of himself now. "And you completely misunderstand Sarrum Arakiel's claim on you. He does not believe you belong to him and though he loves you and will serve you for all eternity, he would never move to stop you from having anything or anyone you wanted. His was a much more permissive culture than you or I were raised in. Though he will never be with anyone but you, he would not, could not, bar you from it."

"Wait, are we talking about blood or sex?"

He raised his head to look at her for the first time since before their bodies touched. "They are the same thing."

"To a vampire, maybe," she argued.

"Vitala take prana more easily from blood, but we can absorb what we need from sex as well. All children of the light feed like Nephilim because we are their children. Each of us have our preferences."

Oren had been "feeding" her and from her since the second he'd changed her. That's why she wasn't hungry. His blood. His sex. "So why are your eyes…like that, and not like Oren's?" Now that his gaze was on her again, she found herself distracted by the black-hole-like pull of them.

"These are the eyes of the vitala. They help me attract…" — he struggled over the next word—"…donors. Only Nephilim have opal eyes like yours. They and their Sinnis', apparently."

Kay's mouth dropped open. How had she gone so long without looking in a mirror? She had opal eyes like Oren now?! She dashed by Hurrit and down the hall to the bathroom. She stared at her reflection and then got close, really close, for an examination. Her eyes were multicolored just like Oren's. They reflected light like they had facets cut into their depths. "Wow."

"Wow indeed."

Kay hadn't seen Hurrit follow her. He wasn't in the mirror. She turned and there he was. She turned back to the mirror and he disappeared again.

He explained quickly, "Old mirrors were backed in silver nitrate. This one must be. Vitala don't reflect in silver backed. Luckily most modern mirrors are backed with aluminum. You are quite lovely. The green hair suits you. I can see why Sarrum Arakiel chose it."

"He didn't choose it. My hair has been green for years. It is a pain to bleach and dye, but I do it because I like it." She leaned in again, this time focusing on her hairline. The roots were green. It was as if it were naturally growing green from her head.

"When he reformed your body after the blood exchange he locked in your image as your true form. He could have chosen any color, length or texture he wanted."

"It's like this forever?"

"It is. Sarrum Arakiel can change it for you anytime you wish, but this will always be your base natural form."

Kay stifled a shriek. No more bleaching and dying for this girl. Hell yeah. She turned to face Hurrit. Running her fingers through his jet-black hair she asked, "So this is the base form that he chose when he made you?"

"No. This is what I looked like when he made me. Making a vitala is a simple blood exchange. There is an extra step when making a Sinnis, one I nor anyone else could have survived. You are something altogether different. That's why I asked you how I smelled. I wanted to see if you reacted like a human or a vitala."

Hurrit had drifted forward toward her as he spoke. She closed her eyes against the onslaught of his energy into her personal space. "And?"

"It was odd. You are entirely human in your reaction to my eyes and teeth, but you desired my blood like a vitala. Your face did not undergo the change that a vitala's does at your hunger. You are like the Sarrum." He took a deep breath, obviously noting the similarities between the scent of her blood and Oren's.

"You need to fucking feed. I can feel your hunger, like a living thing in the room with us."

"That is a more accurate description than you know. At my age, I only need a drop to regain my control and normal appearance, but it is just you and me for miles." He shrugged. "It's not like I can go into town looking like this."

He smiled at her. Those teeth!

"No, I guess not." She returned his smile. Then she had an idea. She grabbed his hand and pulled him down the hall back into the kitchen. There were two man-hand sized chunks taken out of the marble countertop's edge. The snap and crumble sound that had broken the trance Hurrit's blood had her in had been him breaking the marble. She scooped up a basket full of blackberries from under the cabinet that she'd picked with Oren. She turned back to Hurrit with the question on her face.

"You can put those eyebrows of yours down now. Normal food isn't going to do anything for me."

"But you can eat, right? Oren eats sometimes."

"Yes, I can digest but it doesn't nourish m—" She stuffed a blackberry in his mouth, cutting off his sentence.

"Good thing *this* isn't normal food." Kay grinned as Hurrit took the basket from her hand. He stuffed every one into his mouth before the black began to recede back into his pupil, revealing his whites. He smiled at her in amazement. His teeth were stained, but they were the normal human kind again.

"You fertilized with human blood." It wasn't a question. He knew about earth witches and felt foolish for not thinking of this sooner. They wouldn't stave off his need to feed for long, but the fruit took the edge off.

"My own. I was a kid when I tried it the first time, but I made offerings for every plant in my orchard at least once a year after that."

Hurrit nodded his head. He remembered. That was the year that Ki had last spoken to him. She had asked him to make another child of light to watch over a girl who had no one. He was glad Sarrum Arakiel had taught him to hear the mother so that he could carry out her wishes. Tara Kay, his Sarrum Sinnis, his queen, had been that little girl that needed her own guardian vitala.

"I tasted it right after Oren converted me. I had never been able to taste the blood in them until then. I didn't even know what I was tasting until just now when I started thinking about it. I'm glad it works for you though I am a little sorry that you won't hunger for me as much."

Hurrit cursed the gods silently. She was more of a temptation than he could have imagined. He was going to need a lot more fruit before this was all over. They both needed to get their bloodlust under control.

FIVE

Ini-herit Belial Maru.
Nathalia spoke to him mind-to-mind in that split second when she and Eiran were between tabalu and being fully formed. She wasn't sure how she'd be received. Each Nephilim seemed to react to her differently. She never knew what to expect but she didn't expect full-on assault.

She barely dodged the downswing of a Nephilim who seemed intent on splitting her skull. Eiran took her place in the fray. The clang of his metal against another's was startling in the quiet still of the desert. Eiran was much faster than she at pulling the metals in the body and localizing them into a sword. By the time she had her arm reformed into a short sword, the fight was over.

"My apologies. I reacted before thinking." Ini-herit's voice was soft and repentant. He had realized a moment too late that the voice in his head couldn't be from an Akhkharu. The betrayers could no longer tabalu and the sun was still an hour from the horizon. Even in its low position, Ud would burn an Akhkharu in a matter of minutes. "It has been decades since I have even thought my name, centuries since I've heard it from another. My ability is uncontrollable, unconscious, and I have been told it makes my blood irresistible."

Ini-herit paused as if to give them a chance to test his statement. Nathalia looked at him. He was nude, except his birthright necklace, as if it were the most natural thing in the world. His skin was golden, and he glowed more fiercely than any Nephilim or human she'd ever laid eyes on. His wings were tucked behind him, but she could see that they, too, were golden, and not just from the sun. They reflected light as if they were embedded with flecks of gold leaf. His face was regal, large black eyes topped a long thin nose and generous mouth. She could almost imagine him as an Egyptian carving, so broad and straight were his shoulders when compared to his narrow waist and hips. All he was missing was the kohl around the eyes and a staff with an ankh. He was completely hair free, his head the same color as the rest of him. His entire body had a glossy sheen to it that made Nathalia itch to pierce his skin with her teeth.

I am Nathalia Ereshkigal, of the Kafziel family line, chosen warrior of the Shinar, and the living DakuAhu. My hunger and that of my mate are sated and yet we still feel the pull of your blood.

"Keeper of the Betrayers," he said in greeting, "it is good to see you again. You are a Sinnis to this Kafziel Maru, who fights so well?"

Nathalia nodded, smiling proudly at his compliment to her mate. She wondered how Ini-herit knew Eiran when he barely left the betrayers' prison.

"Then they are true, the whispers on the wind. The time of the Sinnis is upon us." He knelt at her feet, offering her his neck, as Eiran had done so long ago. He expected her to kill him, just as Eiran had. "Thank Ud and Ki that my running is over. I am weary. Let the end come silently and the peace after, swiftly."

Ini-herit was no Akhkharu. He had not succumbed to the call of brother's blood. *I am not here for your life. It will not be collected today.* She helped him to his feet, though he shied away from her as soon as he was upright. Old habits died hard. *I need your help.*

"What would the First have of one such as I? You need only speak your will to see it done."

I live in a growing group of women with power, and one recently joined us who has now fallen ill. We can find no reason for it. She and her mother came to us from Ethiopia, and they can call people to themselves, even over great distances. The girl is extremely talented, able to call people she's never met. She even has memories of encounters with what is clearly a Nephilim. I am only wondering if her illness might be linked to her being an unclaimed Sinnis.

"You speak of Minali. Yes, I know her. I confess, when I found her, hope was restored in me that somehow my bloodline had not died out." He unconsciously fingered the stone on his neck at the mention of his bloodline. "We share a similar ability. I too draw people to me, even when I wish I would not. I have been with both she and her mother, and though they attract me, neither is my Sinnis. I do not know how they came by their abilities, but it is not from my maternal line. Not only did I fail to protect the daughters' daughters of my mother, but I had a hand in their lines' deterioration and destruction."

Nathalia itched to plunge her sword hand into him at that last admission. To feel the warmth of his blood, to watch as the thread of life torn from his body and… No. She couldn't. She had promised him that his life would not be collected today, and she wouldn't break her word minutes from making it. Minali needed him. She was concerned only with Minali. For now. Ini-herit might meet his end on the end of her sword one day. *Minali's coven was decimated by an Akhkharu and his abominations. She felt it was her fault. After your last visit, she called for you, longed for you.*

Ini-herit smiled. "I felt her draw. It was hard to resist. She is quite talented."

Why didn't you go to her? Ereshkigal's law said nothing against finding comfort in the arms of humans.

His smile disappeared. "Wherever I go, a trail of murder and destruction follow."

Nathalia was confused. Minali may have thought she brought the Akhkharu that murdered everyone in her community, but Nathalia knew the Akhkharu was after the DakuAhu, the "Kill-Brother." It was a weapon made by her in a past life, out of the bone of a Shinar, bathed in the blood of an unclaimed Sinnis. Was she wrong too? Did Ini-herit have something to do with the arrival of the Akhkharu?

Her thoughts must have been clear as writing on her face, or she could have been accidentally broadcasting them. Ini-herit answered her unspoken questions. "I did not lead any evil to Minali, but because of my visits to her, another place far away was destroyed. Ages ago, when it became apparent that my bloodline, my possibility of love and happiness, were destroyed, I wanted to die. I was angry and ashamed. I fed on the blood of a fellow Nephilim and allowed others to feed on mine. I became Akhkharu. Thank the Great Mother that it was not long before I fell to a Justice Circle. I was many years imprisoned. Many who had tasted my blood never felt the burning justice of Ud's light. When I was released, they gave chase. My brother from another mother is often with them. Every night I fly from them, just fast enough that they cannot stop to harm others or they risk losing me. Every day I sleep with Ud's light to protect and energize me. When I must, I visit humans, feed from them as I did with Minali, but it comes at a great cost."

How do you do it, without bringing an army of darkness with you?

"I lead the hungry pack to as desolate a place as I can find, as unpopulated as possible. Then I tabalu away. They cannot follow and to show their displeasure, they kill everything they can. I do not tabalu often for fear of their recourse. When I went to Minali, confirming, once she was fully mature, that she was not my Sinnis, I left them in the wilderness of North America."

The bear attacks in Canada last year?

Ini-herit nodded solemnly. "Many more died that night than were reported."

Of course, thought Nathalia. The Canadian government wouldn't have wanted a panic. It had happened in the peak of tourist season. *That night, with Minali. Was she… Did her… Would you have recognized if a woman you were with were the Sinnis of another, unclaimed?*

Ini-herit thought about it for a moment. He licked his golden lips. "I am unsure."

"A Sinnis is only recognizable by her Nephilim." Eiran's voice startled them both. As always, his stoic countenance had lulled their awareness of his presence. No one could stand silent watch as Eiran could. In the mother's tomb where they met, Nathalia had thought he was a marble carving for hours before he'd finally moved.

Nathalia accepted Eiran's assessment. He was the only known Nephilim to have ever slept with another's unclaimed Sinnis. He had married Nathalia in her previous life as Ereshkigal, not knowing that she was really his brother's unclaimed Sinnis. She moved on to her next line of questioning. *Have you ever been drained of your powers, only to fall ill physically once they are drained?*

Ini-herit shook his head. "Sadly, no. I long for a day without my ability, even if it brought my death from illness. It would mean the hunting pack would not be compelled to follow me. Minali's condition has nothing to do with her power to call." Then he hissed, looking around frantically.

It was too late. The sun had set while they talked. The hunting pack made of Akhkharu and their beastly children of darkness were upon them. Ini-herit spread his golden wings, bending his knees slightly in preparation of vertical takeoff. Almost as an afterthought he said, "Don't fear. They will follow me away from here. There is nothing as tempting to them as me."

Nathalia put a hand on his wingtip and he froze. *There wasn't anything as tempting before. Now there is: my blood.* She took her sword hand and let it fall on each of her shoulders, making deep cuts there. The wounds bled down her chest and back before closing up. She spread it around, painting her skin, keeping any rivulets from reaching the ground.

He took a step toward her, his eyes locked to the red. Nathalia quickly called on Ki to bind him. He pulled, leaning forward, getting as close to her as possible, barely acknowledging that he was immobilized.

I could kill him now, Nathalia thought. He might not even notice. His prana would warm her birthright and thrill her blood. No. He might be able to help Minali. *They will come to me and I will* end them. *I need you to go to Minali. We need her ability, your ability, to help gather the Nephilim and their Sinnis.*

She broadcasted the Daughters' compound location to him at the same time, notifying Christy that a new Nephilim would need entrance. *Tabalu. The shield will allow you through.*

"You have a shield maker?" Ini-herit asked, clearly excited.

Nathalia nodded. *She protects us and we protect her.* From every side, they could hear the falling of rocks, loosened by the scrabbling of claws and feet of those who answered her blood's call. She wanted them to come to her and they couldn't resist. *Go now. I will meet you on the rooftop.*

He dissolved without argument. She wondered about his interest in Christy. Was it about the girl or her ability? *Hide from them Eiran. They need to think I am unprotected. Be ready to tabalu when I am finished.*

Eiran may not have wanted to obey but he did. When his camouflage covered him completely, even Nathalia could not find him. She waited high on the plateau in the desert. It was cold. How many were there? How would it feel to have all that prana humming through her?

She shivered and waited. Her dream, her vision, came true, unveiled itself before her eyes.

Their monstrous hands came into view first, then their heads and shoulders, until they stood in a ring around her. Their chests heaved with the effort to get to her. Their mouths, filled with stained but razor sharp teeth snapped at her.

They were hairy and large, swollen with the violence and blood they engorged themselves on every night and their ruddy complexion was visible even in the dim light. Every cell in their bodies called for them to flee the desert where there was so little shelter from the sun that would incinerate them, but she was here. They craved her blood more than anything. She was life itself, they thought.

They were wrong. She was death. She was salvation. Nathalia rotated slowly, meeting each unredeemable in the eye.

She spoke, "I am Ereshkigal, Atropos, Beletseri, and Morta. Having broken the promise and feasted on the blood of your brothers, you have lost the ability to control your cells. You are no longer Nephilim, guardians of mankind, but Akhkharu, addicted to violence, and as such you will be the first to die."

These were not the words they were expecting. Her charges against them brought many rushing toward her, but a few turned to run. Both strategies were useless. She called each of them by name, binding them and forcing their lifelines to the surface. The silver threads strained to get to her. Ki held the abominations fast as Nathalia sliced through each line.

Standing still, she savored the collection of prana-carrying lifelines. Their threads of life joining the other she'd collected. She knew their previous owners died around her. She did not care. They did not deserve to live.

The screams of Akhkharu filled the desert as the strings tore from the places they were sewn throughout their bodies. As the silver threads of life unstitched themselves, they came unseamed. It looked for a moment that their blood was boiling, but then as skin broke down, rolling rocks could be seen replacing flesh and bones.

It was over in an instant. As the last prana pulled from them and joined Nathalia's birthmark, their bodies returned to the elements from which they were made. There was a flash as flame ate the air and then a pile of earth laying in a puddle of water was all that remained. One for each of them.

Eiran appeared behind her. She knew, rather than saw. He wrapped his strong arms around her, and she leaned her head back to rest on his shoulder. Nathalia and Eiran vanished into thin air.

OREN SENT Hurrit to work with Kay. He said he had to prepare. For what, he didn't say. Kay tried not to show her disappointment. Hurrit was good company, and she was attracted to him, but he was no Oren. Oren was an irresistible force of nature. Oren had been in her life even before she was born, by existing on her family land, waiting. Hurrit confused her.

She liked Hurrit, felt sorry for his solitude, but she needed Oren. Maybe she even loved him. Their bond was easy to recognize now that she'd seen it, as simple as looking out a window to say if it was day or night. She worried that Oren had grown tired of her already and was passing her off to his friend. It wouldn't be the first time it had happened to her. She convinced herself that wasn't the case. She tried to get through the day, knowing that she would see him tonight after work. After work at her second job, at least.

She served Hurrit his fourth piece, the last, of the blackberry cobbler she'd thrown together before coming to work. The kitchen Oren had remodeled didn't seem to have a stove or oven or anything that got hot, so she'd mixed it up there at home and then cooked it in the big oven at the diner. Hurrit was very interested in the whole process and even more amazed when he found that the berries retained their prana even after baking. Apparently, that wasn't normally the case.

He'd said he needed a plate with pie on it the whole time he was here. He didn't say it, but she knew that her blood was calling out to him. He had paced himself, only taking bites when he absolutely needed to. This piece only had to last until the end of her shift. About an hour more and he could hide in a corner of Bare A$$ets with his lips clamped shut. With what he'd said about blood and sex being the same, Kay wondered if it would be as easy as that in a place like a strip club.

Kay saw a brown uniform and hat come through the door and panicked for a second. She wasn't sure what Sheriff Stout would say nor what Oren had done to him yesterday. The tiny man had an even tinier fuse. He said things to her that big city folk would never believe their lawmen were capable of saying to a young girl. Hurrit could speak English and she doubted that he would tolerate much more than Oren had.

She didn't have to worry. It was just a deputy, not the sheriff. Wayne Rayney was young enough not to have taken part in the raid on her house and her parents' arrest. He was young enough to have known her in school, but too old to have dated. He was resistant to the sheriff's influence where Kay was concerned because he never treated her any differently than everyone else. She wasn't so lucky with the other eleven deputies.

Deputy Rayney strolled right in and, after a quick glance around, plopped down in the last seat at the counter, swiveling so that he faced the door. He put his patrol car laptop on the bar and his hat upside down on that and smiled at Kay. "I hear you baked up some 'a that delicious pie 'a yours. My sources say blackberry even. You know that's my favorite."

"I did. Cobbler, actually. They're right; it's blackberry. And you know I know that. But…"

"Oh, no. Don't say it," he interrupted.

She didn't even slow down but gave him the "sorry" face. "I just served the last piece."

"Damn. I was out on patrol tha whole day or I woulda come 'n get some sooner. Damn it all to hell."

"Better watch your mouth in my place of business, Deputy." Wayne wasn't talking loud but Mr. Glenn had an ear for profanity. He'd come out of his office to collect the register take. He liked to do his figures before closing up for the weekend and get over to the bank before it closed. What little they took in during the last hour on Friday could sit in the store over the weekend. They were almost dead center of town. Thief would have to be plumb nutso to break in there. He could see the courthouse and jail where he'd end up if he tried it.

"Sorry Mr. Glenn," Wayne called out. He leaned in and talked quietly to Kay. "Sheriff was punishin' me 'cause I wouldn't go out and spy on your new friend…the green haired one with the crazy tattoos." Hurrit must have heard that last bit. He subtly perked up. "He said Jackie got video on his phone of you, naked, getting carried off by that naked dude. I told him it's none of our business who you decide to shack up with. He tried to play it off like he wasn't mad but right after that he sent me out and kept the rest of the guys in. They were probably out at your house today. Sorry." He stood to go.

"I couldn't help but hear your disappointment at missing Ms. Tara Kay's blackberry cobbler and I'd like to offer you mine. She served me the last piece and I don't need it. I haven't even touched it yet." Hurrit set the plate down in front of Wayne and didn't wait for an answer before returning to his table.

Wayne looked at it, at Hurrit, and then at Kay. She smiled at him. "It's fine. I did just serve it and he's had three already."

The deputy laughed, sat back down, and dug his fork in. Lifting his first bite high in a kind of salute thank you to Hurrit, he froze for a sec before stuffing it in his face. The vitala just nodded his "you're welcome," glad his plan to keep the deputy here and talking had worked, and went back to pretending to read the newspaper.

Wayne turned his cup right-side up on its saucer and Kay filled it with coffee. After swallowing his first bite and taking his first sip, he started talking again. "Brady says that video was of you doin' satanic stuff. He says that's how Jack, Ash, and Will got themselves so banged up. You called up demons to attack 'em. Then you went off with the devil into the woods. Says it's on YouTube."

Kay started to give him her usual speech about how when small-minded people see something they don't understand they call it witchcraft, but she stopped herself. If this video was out there, Wayne might eventually see it. "It's a movie me and some buddies were making. Ash and the boys are in it, but they decided it would be a better effect if they leaked the footage like it was real. You know to work up some buzz about it. I guess they got the sheriff to go along with it."

Wayne shoveled the next to last bite in his mouth and then laughed, showing Kay a very purple mouth. He swallowed and washed it down with coffee. "I shoulda known. I heard Austin was a big movie-making city."

"It is. That's where I met my movie friends."

He scrapped his plate clean with the edge of his fork, building a bite out of what should have been dish washer fodder. "If the sheriff's not in on it and Ash is pulling his leg, he is going to be in so much trouble. Big city cop came in yesterday and had a meeting with Whitney. I heard it was about you and that guy in that video. Had the boys come into the station too. He's still here so *he* doesn't think it's a movie. It's going to be a big mess if the capital sent someone down over a prank. Maybe it's time for ol' Rayney to get a promotion. Sheriff Rayney, how's that sound to you, Kay?"

She whispered and planted a kiss on Wayne's cheek. "Sounds a fuck-load better than Sheriff Stout, since you asked."

Wayne laughed and looked longingly at his empty plate. Kay thought he might lick it clean. "Delicious as always, Kay. Helluva good way to start the weekend. Making any more?"

"Yes, sir. Barring all natural disasters, there should be a few in on Monday."

"I'll see you for lunch then." He laid a ten on the counter and gathered his stuff.

"It's a date."

He put on his hat and waved over his shoulder on his way out the door. Kay let him get out of view before she went to Hurrit's table. She pretended to be wiping it down as they talked softer than anyone else could hear. "That was some pretty quick thinking."

"How the fuck could Oren let them get away with a tape of his rising?" she asked.

"He doesn't know anything about this modern age and all of its technology. He let the boys keep their memory of it because he doesn't understand how small the world has become. Information travels at faster than light speed. That is not something he is prepared to deal with."

"What the fuck are we going to do?" Oren didn't know that he might be under surveillance right now. He didn't know that the armies of the world could be after him in the blink of an eye.

Hurrit put his hand on the table so that hers brushed it when she swept the rag past. "Don't worry. We'll stick with the movie story. I'll plant some information online. I've become quite good at cover up since Sarrum Arakiel went to ground. Is there an internet café in town?"

Only the seriousness of the situation kept Kay from laughing at the question. This was Calum. The sheriff's office, courthouse, and the library were the only places with computers within a fifteen-mile radius and the one at the library was green screen. "There's one at the club. Crash isn't going to want to let you use it but when we tell him that there's a video out there that shows people for free what he charges them to see, he'll agree."

BARE A$$ETS was packed, even for a Friday night. Crash had his hands full with drunk locals that thought their sixth-generation status gave them the right to act up and claim on the girls. All the quality girls worked on Friday and Saturday night. The week days were a little more iffy. Sunday they were closed, of course. Blue laws were strictly enforced in Calum and the surrounding area. They might have lost the vote to dry the county, but they had the power to restrict when entertainments of "low moral character" were offered.

Tara Kay knew she was considered one of those entertainments of low moral character, but she didn't mind. She had never seen the shame in stripping. The easy nudity of the Daughters of Women had only proven there was no disgrace in sexual acts for public consumption. She might not miss their rules and regulations, but she did miss their lack of prudishness. She supposed she would go back to them someday, but it would be under her own terms.

Most people in her situation would have walked away from a job like this after what had happened to her, like when someone wins the lottery, but Kay didn't mind working. She saw the position in a somewhat sacred light. She was the modern version of temple prostitutes of Inanna, though her temple had undergone some major changes. It seemed kind of dumb when she really thought about it. She also didn't want to worry Melody again by not showing up. She hadn't wanted to be away from Oren, but Hurrit had promised to give her some training while she worked, after he used the office computer to lend credence to her movie story.

The patrons were more worked up than normal and Kay had received her fair share of gropes. Hurrit was taking care of most of the unruly ones. He was a natural bouncer. His presence was intimidating and soothing at the same time. Crash would probably offer him a job at the end of the night. As the evening progressed Kay needed Hurrit to interfere less and less. He was paying for a lot of dances from her and using the time to teach her ways to use her new abilities.

She could now see everyone more clearly. Not just their bodies but their intentions were clear to her. She could smell how intoxicated each one was and sense the location and arousal of each. She was avoiding those she knew would cause her trouble. As always Melody was attending to each of those, putting herself between Kay and any persona non grata.

Tara Kay knew when Ashley, Will, and Jackie came in, even though her back was to the door. She sighed. They always came in on Friday night, so their appearance wasn't shocking. What did stun her about them was the pure malice rolling off of Will, malice that was directed at her. She expected some anger from Ash, but Will had *murder* in his heart. She continued her dance for the sedated balding man whose lap she was grinding. When she looked to Hurrit he was already moving to intercept the three. She turned to look.

Ash still wore his sling, but had it hidden under his leather jacket. Will favored his right foot but walked without his crutches. Jackie's eye was as disgusting as yesterday, maybe more so since it was turning yellow. The courage of all three seemed bolstered despite their battered appearance. They walked through the crowd with a sense of entitlement but that wasn't new. The Stouts and Cunninghams owned this town.

They spoke to Crash and then planted themselves in one of the V.I.P. lounges. Crash gestured to Kay. They had requested her, and he expected her to acquiesce. She went to them willingly. She needed to know what they knew about Oren. They looked smug as she drew the curtain closed behind her.

She stepped up on the tiny, raised dance floor, grabbed the pole, and started dancing. She saw Will reach into his pocket. "Hands where I can see them. You know the rules." She continued her dance, spreading her legs wide and sliding down the pole. "What can I do for you gentlemen tonight?" She barely kept the sarcasm out of her voice when calling them gentlemen.

"I want to see your pink cunt," Will grunted.

"Lap dance," came from Ash.

She kept dancing. She was already scantily clad. "Either or, boys. Make up your minds." She wasn't allowed to grind on them fully nude. Law said she could dance nude as close as three feet away.

"Crash said it was okay." Jackie's voice sounded timid, betraying his insecurity.

Kay just shrugged and looked vaguely apologetic. It wasn't going to happen. She didn't care what Crash had said. He was the one who let Ash sell the dancers drugs. They were the behind the scenes reason this club was so successful. Crash wasn't real big on keeping the law to the letter but she wasn't about to give these guys any special treatment. Not anymore.

Will showed no such signs. "You'll do what you're told, whore."

"As I recall Will, you didn't always think I was a whore. I mean, who proposes to a whore? Oh, didn't he tell you, Ash? After you got arrested it wasn't a week before he tried to take over everything. Your girl, your business, your family, your life."

Will had been sincere at the time. He'd said that he thought he and Kay were meant to be together. He'd even called her Special K. He said that god had told him that she was supposed to be his wife. Kay had avoided laughing in his face but only just. She'd told him that maybe god should have mentioned it to her. Will had eased back on his approach then and asked if she would go out with him a few times so he could show her just how right they were together. She knew that Will was all wrong for her. He had an odd intensity about him. She turned him down flat.

When he'd kissed her, it was aggressive and unwelcome. She'd slapped him hard, leaving her handprint on his face like an ancient red ochre cave painting. "You'd rather be with a criminal who whores you out to his friends? You should hear the way he talks about you. He doesn't love you. He doesn't even like you. He just knows the value of an easy cunt."

She'd recognized the truth when she'd heard it. Sure, she'd had some three ways, even four ways with Ash and the boys, but she'd been into it. She'd never thought of it as anything to be ashamed of until then. Ash had sold her to those other men. He was her pimp. He'd just forgotten to tell her she was a whore. She'd left that week, off to Austin without telling anyone where she'd gone.

"He's the reason I left. He's the reason I was gone when you got out. He said he was your friend, Ash, but the way he acted, I wouldn't be surprised if he was just waiting for you to get arrested." The look on Will's face told her she was getting dangerously close to the truth. She realized something in that moment that she'd never thought of before, something Ash had no inkling of. "Will set you up that night on the interstate. He sent that trooper after you so that he could get to me."

"You *bitch*!" Will lunged at her and if not for her increased reflexes, he would have backhanded her. At the same time Ash leaped up and dove for Will, wrapping his arms around Will's middle. They went down in a heap, all snarling and cursing and punching, taking the curtain down with them.

Her time with them was over before it had really started. Fighting doesn't really go over well in a strip club. It tended to put a dampener on people's good times and their wallets. Hurrit was standing right next to them as soon as Will disentangled himself and stood. "Your time's up, boys," he said through clenched lips. His hunger drive was running on high and he didn't risk exposing his teeth. His sunglasses hid his alien eyes. Startled, Will took a swing at the intruder.

It went wide, catching only air. Ash stood just as Hurrit landed a blow to Will's soft bits, earning an "oof." Ash tried to grab Tara Kay but she moved with her new speed, avoiding him by more than necessary. A flash told Hurrit that the man had tried to cut his queen. That was not to be tolerated. He punched Ash in the face, splitting his skin on the hard unforgiving ridge of the eyebrow and knocking him unconscious.

Hurrit caught the falling, bleeding man and tossed him over his shoulder like a rag doll. He wrapped his other arm around Will's neck, locking him in front. He forced Will to walk forward toward the exit. Hurrit looked back at the still seated Jackie and asked, "You coming nicely or do I need to come back for you?"

Jackie blanched and stood. Hurrit flicked his head forward. He wasn't about to let even a timid man like Jackie behind him. Jackie complied. Crash watched as Hurrit took care of three out of control patrons with awe. He came to stand next to Kay.

"Your boy's pretty damn handy with the rabble."

"Hurrit's not my boy. He's just a friend."

"You might want to tell him that." Crash wondered if the man would become a regular. If the Indian and Special K were dating, Crash might be able to get those stunning bouncer services for free. He doubted he could afford a trained bouncer like Hurrit. "Why don't you do an extra dance on the main stage, and then be as choosy as you want for the rest of the night." Special K was his main pull and keeping her happy was more important than a few customers. "Melody can handle the extra work."

Special K and Melody shared enough features that patrons coming to see the first would settle for the second. They both had pretty faces, big round tits on petite bodies, and narrow waists and hips. Melody was older but had a magnetism to her that, until tonight, Kay couldn't duplicate. Kay was younger and, with that, firmer. She had come back from Austin with a better understanding of her body. Their BDSM show on Monday nights brought in enough money to give Friday competition for highest earner.

"Thanks, Crash." Kay went directly to the DJ booth to put in her request for the last dance. The country rap song got her more cash than any other, but she especially hated it. It was a white guy who couldn't sing, saying words in rhythm with a country twang. Whoever heard of rap with a banjo? But this place wasn't about what she wanted; it was about giving the customers what they wanted so they gave her their money. She had made almost enough tonight already for it to be considered a great take and she really wanted to get home to Oren.

"NOT A word," was all Montana had said. Montana was fairly certain the man back at the club was a vampire. He thought he'd seen the vamp lick the blood off his knuckles. He didn't want the three idiots in the back to say anything that might alert the Native American that they were onto his master. Montana had no idea how good a vampire's hearing was.

Not until they were back at the station, did he free them. The two older ones broke into a fight as soon as the cuffs were off. Montana separated the two brothers from Will. He took the DakuAhu and went in to talk privately to the Cunningham boy.

"What happened?"

Will shook his head. "It was just like you said, only worse. She knew exactly what to say and do to get us fighting each other. Ash had plenty of time to use the dagger."

Montana made a sound that sounded like he understood. "He is weak, and that brother is no better. I should never have trusted him with something so valuable." He clapped the white bone dagger on the metal table between them. "I won't make that mistake again." If he lost the DakuAhu, all hope would be gone with it. Montana shuddered at the thought. It was a risk sharing it with anyone.

Will had an odd look on his face. He stared at the dagger. He started talking without any prompting from Montana. "Before I thought I was just hearing someone in the other room, but I hear it again. Those voices, they're coming from the knife."

Montana didn't stop him when Will reached out and touched the DakuAhu. It took every thread of willpower he had. He could hear it too. Maybe the dagger had a job for Will as well. Holding it was the clearest way to hear its desire. He wondered what the boy would interpret as its meaning.

"They are God. They want blood. They want vengeance. They want what was taken from them." He looked up at the black man across from him. He normally wouldn't associate with them, but this one had something unbelievable. He had a direct line to hear the Lord's voice.

Montana smiled. He was glad Will had a religious background. Men would do much more terrible things to another if they thought their god was behind them. Humans were all too eager to serve gods. "And we will give it to them. That man you fought tonight and the one who was born of a tree, they are both demons. They must be killed, and that knife is the only way to do that, but first it must be bathed in the right blood."

ASH WAS in a foul mood as he drove home. First, he had failed to cut Tara, so Montana was mad. The asshole had even yelled at him. Then Will, who had a beating coming for his role in Ashley's arrest and for trying to take Tara, had stayed with the man who had just yelled at Ash like a child.

He was fuming, vowing to make them both pay. No one spoke that way to him without some serious repercussions. Jackie was smart enough to keep quiet on the drive. He had taken a punch or twenty in the past when Ash couldn't reach the person he wanted to hurt.

Ash parked in front of the house he and Jackie shared and Jackie let out the breath he'd been holding. Once inside they could retire to their separate rooms and Ash could let out his steam on something other than Jackie's face.

Something slammed onto the hood of the car with a crash. They both jumped and then started to scream as a monster smiled at them through the windshield. Its face was not the same color as the rest of its body. Flaming red fur with a spot of white over one ear covered it, reminding them of a fox. This was no fox. This wasn't any animal they'd ever even heard of, much less seen. It roared, and Jackie felt the warm wetness of his bladder emptying itself. Ash had enough of his mental capacity to lock the doors before realizing it wouldn't do anything.

Something else landed on the trunk. A hand, not a paw, hairy and tipped with claws, tore open the roof, rolling it back like the lid of a sardine can. When it was open, the night sky stared down at them. A demon barked an order at the monster on the hood and then turned its terrible attention to the Stout boys.

Its voice was painful, an instrument of torture in and of itself. Ash expected it to say, "I am Legion," the way the one in the bible had. It sounded like a bunch of voices coming from the same mouth. "You will tell me everything you know about the DakuAhu. Then I will decide if your memories are to be erased or if, because of your attempt on the life of a Sinnis, you need to die."

SIX

Tara Kay tried not to talk about Oren all the way home. It was hopeless. She was so anxious to see him and hear his voice that she couldn't help it. Hurrit didn't seem to mind. He even joined in the praises of his king's attributes. Hurrit loved him too. He understood how she felt. Maybe it was just a progeny/maker thing, but Kay doubted that. She doubted that Hurrit could be apart from Oren for all that time if he felt like *she* did about the Nephilim. It had only been a day and she was aching for him.

"I like this road." Hurrit changed the subject. He would speak to Sarrum as soon as possible, make sure Arakiel was aware of Tara Kay's feelings.

Rural Route 4, on which her house was box 221, was a beautiful drive. It was blacktop with no center stripe. Barely wide enough to be two-way, she knew that around any turn she might have to take to the dirt to avoid a collision. The trees that grew on either side of the road were thick and their branches joined overhead to make a canopy of green that had graced the cover of Texas Monthly more than once. "I do, too. Always have."

Tara Kay ventured a glance over at him. He was much more composed since his encounter with Ash and the boys. His hunger was sated, his eyes and teeth back to normal. She wondered if he'd fed on them out in the parking lot. Never one to hold her tongue, Kay asked him.

He hadn't, not really. He'd only licked his knuckles clean. He'd wanted to question them, but the sheriff's deputy had gotten there too fast. They must have been in the area. Or maybe there was always trouble on Friday night at Bare A$$ets.

Hurrit helped the deputy and the un-uniformed man get the three into the car. It was the other man who had Hurrit worried. He hadn't had a badge, but just reeked of authority. That was a ruthless man used to getting what he wanted. The boys had been cuffed but not searched even though Hurrit had told the deputy that he thought Ashley had a knife. Something else had bothered him about the situation. No one had read the boys their rights.

The night was comfortably cool, and Kay had the windows down as they drove. She enjoyed the smell of home. It was so moist and green and full of life. "Do you smell that?" Hurrit nodded, his head already turned out of the window. "Is it…blood?"

Hurrit took a deep breath as they pulled to a stop near her house. "Yes, human. Three, maybe four dead or dying." They opened their doors at the same time. "I'll investigate after you are safely in the Sarrum's arms."

The blood was much closer than her tree. She knew how fast she could move and wasn't afraid. If there were three or four dying people close to her, she was taking her magic to try and help them. She found herself in the orchard seconds after she'd decided that's where they were. Hurrit was on her heels.

"We don't know what did this. There are things that go bump in the night that you know nothing about. It could be a trap."

Kay didn't hear him. The scene was gruesome. Moonlight shone down on what looked like an animal attack. Body parts littered the orchard's central clearing, too many to be from just one person. Ages and sexes were impossible to determine, strewn as they were.

"Look out!" a voice called, and Kay turned just in time to see a giant beast charging toward her and Hurrit. Hurrit cursed in the ancient language he and Oren shared, while putting himself between his queen and the monster. The beast changed direction and went after the voice that had warned them of its attack, and Kay got her first good look at it.

It had the profile of a wolf, but its proportions were off. More the size of a grizzly bear, it ran on four limbs that dug deep gouges out of the earth. She knew by looking that it could walk just as easily on two and that each arm or leg ended in huge claws. Its muzzle was big and dark, dripping with the blood of its kills. Her superhuman vision told her something was off about the animal, but she didn't have time to think what.

A man's scream tore through her. The man who'd warned her was being torn apart the way these others had been. The sound stopped with a crunch and gurgle. Kay ran around Hurrit and found the man in what couldn't have been more than three strides.

He was bad off. Dying but not yet dead. The beast had destroyed his face, neck, and stomach, maybe not pausing at all, but just trampling over him, gouging his body the way it had the earth. The man could have been someone she knew, but it was impossible to tell. "Save him!"

She cursed at Hurrit when he just stood there. Sinking to her knees beside the shredded man, she plunged her hands into the blood-soaked soil. She didn't know how to do this. She wasn't a healer and she had no one to help her. She begged silently.

You always have us. We can help you, child. There was the woman's voice. It was so much clearer than it had ever been. *You are our chosen. You and your family will hold this place against the Shinar when they come.* She didn't know who the Shinar were, and she certainly didn't have any family to speak of. Then a calm feeling settled over her. She knew what to do. This man would be the first in her family. She, like Oren before her, would make an army of progeny to protect the family land, just as Oren's watched over their family bloodlines.

Kay manually lengthened her incisors with less concentration than she would have expected it to take, and bit through the skin on her wrist. Hurrit moved then. He grabbed her arm, keeping it from raining down on the broken man.

"He has the stink of Akhkharu on him. It's old but there nonetheless. He could be dangerous." He released her hand when his Sarrum Sinnis growled at him, exposing her teeth. It was obvious that his queen would do as she wanted. He released her arm. He was holding it gently; she could have pulled away from him if she'd wanted. "I only want you to be prepared. If he comes back... wrong...he will have to be destroyed. Ki chooses those she would have as her children and I have not heard her voice."

"I have. Kiyahwe would have me make him." He would be her first, her Hurrit.

She dribbled a little bit of her blood onto the wounds of his stomach before the bite marks closed up. She calmly took another bite, this time tearing away the tender flesh, making a large wound. The blood flowed more freely, and she donated generously to the dying man. When the wounds on his neck and stomach started to close, she put her attention to his face.

Angling her arm so that the blood flowed down her fingers, she traced inside the deep claw marks with her fingertips. She squeezed the gaps together once the muscles had started to repair and spread even more blood over the skin. She didn't want the man to be forever scarred.

"He must consume the holy blood if he is to be made," Hurrit instructed from behind her.

Pressing the now closing wound over the man's mouth, she prayed to Kiyahwe that he would live. At first the blood just trickled down his throat but as he began to draw from her and swallow, she recognized his face. With him pulling from her, she didn't care that he was Billy, her friend from the Daughters of Women compound. Hurrit had said she shouldn't give blood because she didn't know what it would do to her. She knew now. It was intense. She was weighted down with a blanket of need. "Oren. I need..."

Hurrit knelt behind her. He wrapped one hand around her waist, pressing her back against him. "I know. I know, my queen. If you would allow it, I can provide what you need."

She didn't answer verbally but made a soft whimpering sound in her throat and ground her hips back into Hurrit. It was confirmation enough for the vitala. Sarrum Arakiel would need to replenish her later, but Hurrit could give her release. He was just serving her, not taking advantage. It would be hard to resist doing what he really wanted to her, but he had plenty of practice in restraint. Six thousand years of it.

He put his other hand on the top of her thigh and slid up her sun dress. She parted her legs for him and laid her head back on his shoulder. He tried not to look at the curve of her neck or the pale blue vein just below the surface.

Sweet goddess, she smelled good.

He closed his eyes and held his breath. Vitala didn't really need to breathe anyway. It was more of habit than anything else. He cupped her mound and felt that her panties were already soaked. At least this torture wouldn't last long with her as enthralled as she was because of the feeding.

The beast plowed back into the clearing, headed right for them. Hurrit and Tara Kay didn't notice. Oren appeared between them and the monster. It refused to cower when faced with death. Oren punched the creature. While it was down his arm shimmered, changing shape and substance. He brought his sword hand down on the neck of the vrykolak, severing its head.

Kay reached her hand back over her shoulder and tugged Hurrit's face to her neck. His kisses along her pulse and ear were guarded at best. He couldn't do what she was asking because he wasn't sure she understood what she was offering. She had lost a lot of prana saving the man lying in front of them. He wouldn't take more from her with the thrall muddling her mind so thoroughly. She angled her face up to his and he kissed her hard on the mouth. That closed lip press was enough to send her over the edge. As shudders rocked his queen's body, Hurrit held her tight, determined that no one, not even himself nor his Sarrum, would hurt her.

THE LIBRARIAN didn't wait for Maeve and Camilla to get to her before she announced, "It's mate-sickness." Libby made her diagnosis, but nobody breathed a sigh of relief. Maeve and Camilla looked at each other. "That's a good thing for Minali, easily fixed." Libby pressed, wanting a better reaction.

Maeve plopped down in the chair opposite Libby at the reference table. The elder woman had called in the Abbess and healer as soon as she was certain. The giant tome on the table was old and probably the reason Libby hadn't brought the news to them. Camilla lowered herself down on a nearby ottoman. It was much more her size and it was padded for her weary pregnant ass.

"If her mate's alive, it easily fixed." Maeve knew about mate sickness. All matchmakers did. It was part of their training. But with the virtual shrinking of the world, with the worldwide internet and supersonic jets, it was unheard of in this day and age. When Maeve worked her magic there were several sub-spells: the bridge, the call, and the recognition. A person got mate-sick when they received the call spell but was not physically able to go to their mate, who would have only the recognition spell. It happened a lot when people's movements were more restricted or slow. "There isn't much that can keep a called mate away. Death being the most obvious."

If Minali's mate died after the spells were cast but before meeting her, then the outlook for Minali was not good. It was similar to what happened when half of a mated pair died after years of being together. The other half wasted away, but at least they had the memory of a love so deep it was killing them to be apart. Minali had nothing to hold on to.

"That's just it. Minali is suffering because she's the called mate. Her mother's ability is too powerful; it's keeping Minali from answering the call. Her mate only has the recognition spell. He, or she, can only recognize her; they can't come to her because they don't know where she is." Libby was never more animated than she was when she'd discovered something in her books.

She spun the text around so that it was right side up for Maeve. "It's all right here." She pointed out the relevant passage. It was printed on a press with movable type in English, putting the event about a hundred years earlier. It confirmed Maeve's thoughts that it didn't happen often in modern times.

"What do we do?" This from Camilla, ever focused on the end result. The healer had to get her patient well; she wasn't used to being useless. Even Nanae, who was unencumbered by her ability's specifications, with his near limitless abilities had been able to do nothing for Minali.

"I can matchmake for Minali. We'll leave it up to her," Maeve decided.

Camilla shook her head. "Slipped into a coma." They wouldn't be asking her anything.

Maeve rubbed her forehead with open palm, closed her eyes and pinched her lips together anxiously. The decision fell to her, as it often did now that she was Abbess, and she didn't have long to deliberate. Not now that Minali had gotten this bad. "I'll do it and hope that her mate isn't being held by pirates or something. If I don't, we'll lose Minali anyway. It still might not happen in time to save her." She stood. Better now than later. It was a risk to Minali's unacknowledged mate. They could end up in the reverse situation with the mate being unable to come to Minali and then they'd both die.

BILLY BECAME aware that he was not alone. He was the subject of an argument.

"If you take another god-damned step, fuck-all good Oren will do you. I will cut you from crown to cunt if you try to hurt him, Hurrit. I don't care how fine your ass is or how well you stroke the little man in my canoe."

Billy smiled. Only one woman he knew used that kind of language on a regular basis. He pulled his longtime friend and sometimes lover, Special K, against him. The move solicited a warning from Kay that was more of an "un-uh" than real words, but it wasn't directed at him. She was keeping someone from pulling them apart.

In a flash of red violence, he remembered. The women, the beast, the blood, the pain; it all came rushing back to him. He crab-walked back against the headboard and tried to get his eyes to adjust. Kay was there in a heartbeat, her hand on his chest, soothing him.

"Where di…wha…good goddess, what was that thing?"

"It was a dark vrykolak." A man's voice answered him with a smooth cadence that put him at ease even though Billy didn't understand what it meant. "Now you must answer the questions of Sarrum Arakiel Maru."

"Oren!" Kay jumped up from the bed and ran straight into the arms of a giant. A green haired, tattooed giant picked Kay up and held her against his chest like an infant. The way he kissed her was nothing like how one treats a baby, though.

"I thought that all the Nephilim were gathering around Austin. What are you doing way out here? Shouldn't you be protecting the One? The others have sworn their allegiance to her already, or so my mom tells me." They all three just stared at him so he continued. "You've been gone forever, Kay. So much has happened. You really should have returned my calls. Or at least Ingrid's calls. She's your Primo, for goddess sakes. She's been worried sick. She's why I'm here. I left the compound like six months after you did. I've been backpacking around the country for almost a year and Ingrid called me and ask me to look in on you."

"Enough! Before you can be allowed access to the queen, we must determine what you are." The dark skinned, dark haired man's voice was out of this world. The giant still had not spoken.

Billy's laugh rang out. "I don't know what's funnier—you wondering 'what I am' or that Special K is your queen."

Hurrit ignored him. "Do you hunger for anything?"

Billy shook his head no.

"Look at Sarrum Sinnis Tara Kay. What does she make you want? Raw meat, blood, sex?" If the Native American hadn't looked so serious, Billy would have laughed again.

"I'm a vegetarian. Haven't had a bite of meat in …" He paused to think. "…twelve years, maybe? And as for sex…" He gestured to his crotch. "…no action there since Maeve worked her matchmaking magic on me. She warned me it might not work with other women until I found my mate, but I didn't take it as seriously as it obviously was. I have no desire for anything, really."

The Indian spoke to the giant in a foreign language. Kay jumped down and bounced over to Billy. "So, why'd you leave? Nathalia pull that Abbess' orders shit on you too?"

"Actually no. She died. She came back though, kinda like I just did, I guess. She disappeared for a while and then came back with a Nephilim of her own. She calls herself Ereshkigal of the Kafziel family line. Her magic is crazy powerful now. I left because I tried to kill her. I mean, not on purpose. I ran into an Akhkharu and it poisoned my brain and tricked me into stabbing her because she was his Sinnis in a previous life and she'd chosen his brother as her mate both times." He ran his hand through his hair. The two men in the door were looking at him as intently as Kay was. "None of this is coming out right. Too much has happened for me to just tell you in one sitting. Plus everything's getting filtered through my mom. I sound like a crazy man."

"Hurrit!" Kay exclaimed as the man had tugged Billy into a standing position. "He's not ready yet."

"Actually, I feel great. I'd like to go outside." Billy looked down at her. He suddenly had a terrible urge to go home, as if seeing her made him homesick. He hoped he could convince her to go with him when he went back to Austin.

Hurrit nodded at him. "The night is calling to you. Annu is full and high and waiting."

They left without another word.

"I wish you could tell me what the fuck just happened," Kay complained. "But at least you're here now. I missed you."

Oren stood in the doorway staring at his Sinnis. "TeRAkay, you are the most beautifully alive woman I have ever seen. You glow. You are the reason to breathe again as well as the air in my lungs and earth at my feet. I am fortunate to have lived long enough to meet you and will be honored to serve you for the remainder of my none too short life."

Kay grinned. "You certainly mastered English fast. That was a pretty damn impressive speech."

It was Oren's turn to smile. "I learned from the fucking best."

SEVEN

Kay made a salad for Billy. Oren said that her progeny would be hungry when he got back if he hadn't already taken down a deer. That's when she'd decided to make him a salad. Billy wasn't going to eat venison. Especially not raw. She threw together a nice raspberry vinaigrette using her best batch of raspberry preserves.

The minute she was finished, Oren had her in his lap. He palmed the back of her head and pressed it to his bare chest. With the pinkie nail of his other hand, he made a small incision in his skin under her mouth. He pressed her to it without letting her hunger rise.

Kay made three draws before the wound closed up. The blood was much too delicious for that to be it. She had given a lot to Billy. She opened wide and pierced his skin with her own teeth. Oren sat silently as she suckled but his erection was shouting his feelings loud and clear. His blood was heaven, and she took it down in great gulps letting it flow over her tongue slowly. He kissed her when she was finished.

"He is vrykolak. Sarrum, her blood has done the impossible. She's made a child of the light with no more hunger than a human. He doesn't suffer from the beast at all, and he can change at will." Hurrit was in the kitchen before the front door had even slammed.

"He's a vrykolak... the same as that monster that attacked us?" Kay asked, forcing the slur from her speech.

"No, not the same. Your child is not tainted by the hunger beast. That thing in the orchard is all hunger beast. It has lost whatever part of itself that used to be human. A dark vrykolak feeds on violence and murder. It is bound to its most terrible shape. Billy has full control over his shift."

"He's a shape-shifter? A fucking werewolf?" Kay shook her head in disbelief. "My blood did that to him?"

Oren smoothed the hair back from her face. "That and much more. Your blood has done something never done before. It has taken the shit parts of being a child of light or dark and given only the strength and life. That is why my first is so goddamned excited. He and his kind have suffered under the weight of the hunger but your blood, freely offered, could end all of that."

Kay spoke to Oren. "I've offered it to him repeatedly, but he won't take it." She turned to Hurrit who now knelt on the floor. "I know how powerful it is. I know what it feels like to give. I know what the blood does. Will you just grow a pair and bite me, Hurrit?" She laughed but wished she hadn't.

Hurrit looked up at her with his solid black eyes, his hunger full on him yet again, and nodded. He didn't bite immediately when she got close enough to offer her neck to him. He let his hunger rise, enjoying the feel of it, the strength of it, for the last time. He was shaking and his appetite hadn't yet crescendoed fully. He knew what would whet his whistle.

He held his hands only an inch from her body, a question in his eyes. Kay noted that he was asking her and only her. He wasn't asking Oren if it was okay. He understood that she belonged to no man, and so did Oren. His queen smiled at him. "If it's gonna be like it was with Billy, I'm gonna need some petting."

Hurrit ran his hands along the curves of her body savoring the soft material of her dress and skin. Suddenly Oren was pressed against her back. Kay reached over her shoulder, expecting to run her fingernails over his chest, but met his shoulder instead. He was kneeling behind her just as Hurrit was kneeling in front. Oren was so tall that in this position he was closer to her height, only one foot taller instead of three. He traced the soft skin of her inner arm from elbow to pit, leaving a trail of fire along the way, before cupping her breast. His giant palm made her double Ds look almost small.

Kay's intake of breath was the only sound in that kitchen. Hurrit slipped the strap of her dress off her shoulder, pulling it down to reveal the other magnificent breast. He had seen her, of course, at the club where she danced but was unprepared for the experience up close. Perfectly round, slightly too large for her delicate frame, but still perky; those milky white mounds with dainty pink nipples were exquisite. They had the same blue veins that marked the rest of her, though here they were even more visible, even the smallest ones.

He traced the subtle lace with his tongue. He could almost taste her prana through her skin. He wanted it but not bad enough. He wanted the desire to hurt before he banished it forever. He nuzzled the soft white skin with his sun-darkened face, rubbing back and forth over the even softer pink areola and nipple with his cheeks and mouth. He flicked it with the tip once, then twice, before laving at it with the flat of his tongue. He blew on it, pleased when it hardened into a hard pink peak. There on the edge of the tiny goose bumped area was an especially thick blue line. That was where Hurrit would take from.

He thought about how soft she would be in his mouth, how sweet she would taste, how the sound of her soft moans and sweet pussy smell would fill the kitchen as the thrall set on and he knew he had waited long enough. He was more excited than he'd ever been, just from one breast of his queen. He felt Sarrum Arakiel move his hand between them. His maker pulled Kay's dress up and slipped her panties down so that he could get at her flooding folds. The aroma of her arousal was perfume to Hurrit's nose.

"Yes," she whimpered. She was speaking to both of them while watching Hurrit's face as he opened his mouth and prepared to take her into his mouth. He took a deep breath, putting every detail to memory. He waited until Oren had brought the flush of climax to her face before sliding his teeth through her thin skin.

All reasonable thought left his brain when her prana hit his tongue. Instantly, permeating his every cell, it was like his first drink of the Sarrum, only better. Sweeter. For a moment he heard Tara Kay's moans and then the voice of the great mother, Ki, came through as clear as any time previously.

This is my blood, which is given to you. This is my chosen daughter, my vessel. So then, whoever drinks of her blood in an unworthy manner will be guilty of sinning against my body and my blood and they will not find peace in the feast. They that would drink ought to examine themselves before taking from my vessel. For those who drink bring my judgment on themselves. Nevertheless, when you are judged in this way, you are being disciplined so that you will not be taken at the final coming of the Shinar. So then, my sons and daughters, when you gather to eat, you should all eat together. Each year you shall gather together to feast on her blood and through her, and only through her, you shall revel in my word. This is my will and you, first son of the first son, will ensure it is carried out as I would have it.

The door slammed and Hurrit came back to himself. He suckled gently as the puncture holes he had made in his queen, the chosen vessel of the great mother earth, healed themselves closed. He placed a dozen reverent kisses on her bosom worshipfully.

"Whoa, wow. Geez, sorry to interrupt." Billy was standing in the kitchen opening staring at the ménage à trois.

All three of them had heard the mother, though her words had been addressed only to Hurrit. Kay was in the throes of the afterglow and that, added to hearing a goddess' voice, was a heady mix. She couldn't struggle through the fog to speak. She thought of Billy. She thought of how it had felt to give him her blood and of all the times they'd had sex. She motioned that Billy should join them.

Oren laughed in a large jolly way that sent shivers down Kay's spine. He found it amusing that her bloodlust was insatiable and she was unabashed about it.

"Not that I wouldn't love to, but I just came in to tell you that the police are here." He wasn't happy about their appearance. Some of the men smelled *off* to him and his new nose but he didn't know how to interpret what he was sensing. At least they saved him from having to admit that even in the presence of such a sexual fantasy, his equipment just wasn't cooperating.

SHERIFF WHITNEY Stout was waiting for them when they reached the orchard. The sun wasn't breaching the horizon, but its light was. It exposed a gruesome sight behind the visibly shaken sheriff with the feminine name. Oren, who had insisted on carrying her, set Kay down near Whitney but stood even closer. He wouldn't risk this man with a golden star on his shirt grabbing his Sinnis again.

Unable to shake the effects of Ki's words, Hurrit had stayed behind. He had so much to think about. His life, his mission, unchanged for thousands of years, had just switched tracks. Billy had stuck with the vitala. They were still uncertain about his control around so many people, no matter how he protested that he wasn't a danger. He hadn't wanted to let Special K get too far away from him and was puzzled by the feelings. Hurrit had said it was natural to feel protective of one's maker.

The sheriff got out his notebook and pencil. It wasn't often that Rusk County sheriff's department had a triple homicide to investigate, and he didn't intend to botch this one. He needed notes when he talked to the two prime suspects. "We got an anonymous call a while ago saying there had been some people killed in a satanic ritual on the witch's property north of town. You're the only witch I know so we came out here and find this in your orchard. Can you tell me just what the hell happened here, Miss Woods?"

Kay shook her head and shrugged, though her eyes were glossy with tears. "Looks like some kind of animal attack to me. Maybe a bear? I heard some people at the diner talking about seeing a pack of bears."

"In east Texas?" He looked at her suspiciously.

"Well yeah. It looks like they were torn apart. See the jagged edges and massive bite and claw marks? No man could do that," she reasoned.

"Maybe a woman with the right tools could make it look like an animal did it."

"A wom... you mean me? I'm a suspect? I couldn't have done it. It happened while I was at work."

"You seem to know an awful lot about this mess not to be involved."

She did know a lot. She knew that there was one giant vrykolak's body missing but mentioning it would place her at the scene of the crime. "Call Crash. Or better yet just ask your sons...or Will. They were there."

"I know they were, but *he* wasn't." Whitney poked his thumb in Oren's stomach. "What do you think, Will? This guy weighs what, four hundred pounds, four fifty? A team of horses can draw and quarter a man. I bet a couple big guys like this could manage it," he called to Will, who was standing next to a tall black man in a suit. They were as far from Oren and Kay as possible while still being in the scene. Will looked green. He didn't bother to answer.

The coroner and his assistant arrived then. They drove their specially made hearse right up to the crime scene. They made a big show of putting on their paper suits, masks, and gloves. Kay thought they looked old, like they ordered all that stuff years ago and this was their first chance to use them. They got out a couple body bags but after seeing the state of the bodies, exchanged them for smaller bags of varying sizes and shapes.

Oren must not have realized what they were for until they started to put a severed leg into one. "No. They must remain on the earth. Mother will take them into her bosom."

Kay put a hand on his arm when he made a move toward the men. "Oren, they have to take them, identify them, and determine the cause of death. They have families that must be notified." He didn't move so he must have understood the need to remove the bodies, but he never took his eyes off of their actions. He didn't like it. What thinking person would take a body from the earth and encase it in man-made plastic! Contact with the soil brought them peace.

The sheriff watched the giant watching the bloody carnage. "I'm afraid you're gonna have to come with me back to the station to answer some questions, Mr. …." He waited but the man paid him no attention. "You're not from around here, are you? See, around here, I'm the law, and when I ask you a question you damn well better answer me real quick. I'll extend you a courtesy and ask you again just in case you didn't hear me. What's your name, boy, and where'd you come from?"

Kay elbowed him. Oren turned to the small man. "You may call me Sarrum Oren Arakiel Maru, and I have roots in this area."

Kay choked on a laugh and started coughing. Sheriff Stout eyed her and then turned to Oren. He narrowed his eyes to slits. "Roots around Calum? Not with a name like that you don't. Sounds like a terrorist name to me." A few deputies had started to close around them as they talked. Several of them had their guns out, hanging at their sides.

Kay shook her head and warned them. "I wouldn't if I were you."

Whitney took out his cuffs, then thought twice, and put them back in his holster. He didn't think they would fit around this guy's wrist anyway. "Just come in quietly and nobody has to get hurt." Three deputies leveled their weapons.

Oren started to sing.

It was just like when it happened at the diner. Everyone stopped what they were doing and looked at Oren. It wasn't every day that a giant with an out of this world voice busted out into song in a foreign language. Starting with the sheriff, Oren made eye contact with each of the men. They each went back to what they were doing, sans pointed guns and suspicions. The crime scene photographer exposed all his film and Whitney tore the page he'd been writing on in his book, put it in his mouth, chewed it, and swallowed it. Oren finished his song and scooped up Kay. He left, and the sheriff shouted after them, "Thank you for all your help! We will be off your property as quick as possible."

SHE WAITED until they were back inside the house with Hurrit and Billy before she asked, "Where did the body go? The monster you killed."

"Disappeared when the sun rose as all bodies of children of darkness do."

He seemed to dismiss it, so she accepted it as a closed conversation. She had more pressing questions. "What the hell is that you keep doing to the sheriff?"

"What?" Billy and Hurrit said in unison.

Oren stood Kay up on her own two feet and put his hands on her shoulders. He thumbed her neck. "We were in deep shit. Fucking guns pointed at us. They, of course, think we ritually massacred those people and then ol' Pavarotti over here starts up."

Billy looked confused but Hurrit said, "Ah, yes. His song." He gestured to the chair and Kay sat. She suddenly felt very tired. Today had already been one helluva day, and it was only 9 a.m. Oren went behind her chair to continue her massage. Hurrit knelt in front of her and took her hand. Insides up, he laced his fingers into hers. With his thumbs he rubbed her palms. Kay closed her eyes. She didn't know what they were doing but all her tensions melted away. She could get used to being treated like a princess.

Oren spoke softly so that he penetrated her tired mind without shattering her relaxation. "Each of us have an individual talent, something none other can do, but all Nephilim share a few abilities. We live forever. We are incredibly strong and near impossible to kill. We can camouflage our appearance so that it is impossible for a human to remember what we look like or what we say. What you see is not how I looked as a young adult. This is how I choose to appear. My natural form is not one that would fit in a crowd."

Kay didn't like the thought that she didn't really know what Oren looked like. "Show me. I've seen Hurrit's face all vamped out. I can take it."

"Another time, my love."

She was about to object when Hurrit jumped in. "His true form, like his true name is his most guarded secret. It isn't you he hides it from but Billy and I."

Billy raised one shoulder and dropped it. He smirked at her. He seemed to be taking all of this in stride. "What else?" he asked as he crossed to the door. He wouldn't take part in the Kay worship, but he could keep watch. Those policemen were a little close to let down his guard yet, not to mention the monster that had attacked him was still on the loose.

"Just flight and song. Our song can take the memories of humans. In men, we can replace them with those of our choosing. We can erase anything we deem dangerous. With the lawmen, I just took their memory of our conversation, their suspicions of me, and replaced them with a general feeling of me giving all the right answers. I overwrote with the impression of cooperation and innocence."

"Have you ever done that to me? Overwritten my memories?"

"No. Absolutely not. I could have blocked your memories when you were human, but the female mind is more sophisticated than the males. It is difficult to completely erase and impossible to overwrite. I cannot even block your memories now that your conversion is complete."

"Because I'm not human anymore." It wasn't a question. Enough had happened to her that she had no doubt that she was superhuman. Her blood was some kind of magical elixir, for goddess sakes.

"What's your special ability then?" Billy asked from his sentry position.

Kay had a suspicion it had to do with his sinfully seductive mouth.

"I, like all of the Arakiel family line, speak to the Great mother Ki, who hears and answers." Oren began to finger through her hair. He used his nails to part it and his fingers to weave it. Kay could feel every strand, alive and humming with pleasure at being given the task of holding such an elaborate style.

"You're an earth witch, like Special K. You know Kay, the Daughters' garden was really struggling after you left. I bet it's totally fallen into ruin now that I'm gone too. Ingrid's skills lie in mixing up the herbs, not growing them."

Hurrit spoke up. "You're a witch too? You make offerings to the Mother and she answers?"

Billy shook his head. "No. The only offering I ever made was my time. Without that and Kay's special blood offerings, I'm sure they are struggling. We should go back soon, Kay."

It was Tara Kay's turn to shake her head no. "You go. Wouldn't do any good for me to go back. My powers are gone. Taken. Along with all the witches in the SOFE coven. I can't remember exactly what happened. It's been coming back to me in pieces. There was a lot of blood and light and then the pain of my ability being pulled from me."

"Holy shit, Kay. That's terrible. I really want to go home. But I can't go back without you. I feel…compelled to stay and …protect you. Sounds dumb seeing as you are sandwiched between two of the most powerful beings I've ever seen, but it's the truth." Billy saw that smile cross Kay's face that said she was imagining herself sandwiched between Hurrit and Oren like she'd been earlier in the kitchen. He wondered how long it would take her to get back in that position. "Hey, wait. Have you tried to use your ability since Oren gave you his blood? It's got healing properties, right? Maybe it healed your ability." He sniffed the air. "You'll have to test the theory later. Men are coming. Three, maybe four." He smiled. "Nothing Hurrit and I can't handle."

EIGHT

Montana was nervous. He was walking right into the den of a Nephilim with a newly found Sinnis. That Nephilim would likely not hesitate to kill to protect her, but Montana had to know if she had been claimed or not. If she was still human, she wouldn't have any problem giving over a blood sample. If she was converted Sinnis, there could be trouble for him even asking for it.

He was in charge. He'd brought the sheriff along to work as a kind of litmus test for the Nephilim's attempted mind control. Montana needed to know when the giant was using his ability and the sheriff would be able to show him how he should be acting. Will was there too but Montana had trained him, given him the secret for protecting his mind. He wasn't sure of the younger man's acting ability and so Will had been instructed to stay outside. He knew Will was glad for the order that would keep him in the safe zone. Will also held the DakuAhu. The boy was developing quite an attachment to the dagger.

Montana raised his hand to knock, and the door opened before he could. Outwardly he handled it well, but inside it took him a minute to re-compose himself. Staring him in the face was the oldest vampire he'd ever seen. Montana didn't know about the other man. It was hard to tell, they both looked so normal, but Montana had been trained to recognize the signs. He had been in charge of obtaining the Lilitu Brian had needed for his experiments. Brian had created a tranquilizer from her blood that could take down a Nephilim. How Montana wished he had a clip full of that stuff in his gun. As it was, he only had two doses, not enough in a room full of the Nephilim's children. He was glad the dart gun was tucked away in his back holster.

"Excuse me for intruding but is Miss Woods here?" Neither man answered. He knew this was her house. The sheriff was more than convinced she was living in the condemned building even though he had evicted her parents over a decade ago and given her numerous personal warnings of the dangers of living in a home that dilapidated. It didn't appear dilapidated at all anymore.

"There is a large amount of blood at the scene, as would be expected from the level of violence but I'd like to get DNA samples in order to scientifically eliminate Miss Woods and her associate from the suspect list." It was a good story, and he was sticking with it. He might be able to make more tranq serum if he could get blood from either of the men before him, but the look on their faces said he wasn't getting it.

Finally, the vampire spoke. "She's sleeping. It took a lot out of her, seeing those people torn apart that way."

"Of course. We'll come back at a more convenient time." A lot of good it would do him. Montana knew that these two would never let him or any other unknown close to that woman. To try was to die. He was greatly outnumbered. He wasn't sure how to remedy that. He needed to grow his ranks, but the pickings were slim around here.

Montana tried to make backing down the porch steps look natural. The last thing he needed to do right now was trigger the hunting instinct in these two ultimate predators.

BACK IN the car, following the sheriff's closely, Will fought the shakes and worked up the courage to ask Montana, "Did they slaughter those people?"

The man made a noise that could be interpreted as affirmative.

"Why?"

Montana had killed those four women. The DakuAhu needed their magic blood. He didn't know what had torn up their bodies like that. He'd left them in the orchard as the dagger had told him. It didn't matter. He said what he had to in order to gain what he wanted. "She's evil. Those men with her are killers. It's too late to save her as I planned. They're all demons doing the devil's work. It is our job to stop them."

Mercifully he didn't ask how. Montana wasn't sure. He needed a military based faction, like the one he and Brian had started from the ranks of their own service years. Maybe a few teams of experienced fighters could distract those two monsters and their maker long enough for Montana to get some of the woman's blood on the DakuAhu.

He needed to work with what he had, but what he had was nothing. There were no Paion within one hundred miles. He might be able to get some men from Dallas, but the last he'd seen of them hadn't left him with any confidence in their abilities. They were a superstitious group, obsessed with the mythology, like the religious locals of this humid woodland.

He'd hit on something with that line of thought, and he actually pumped the vehicle breaks. He needed to use what he had, and what he had wasn't nothing. It was a whole lot of easily influenced religious zealots with not much more in their lives than taking on the imagined "attack on 'Merican values" that their faux news told them was happening. He could give them more than just an imaginary threat. They had the real thing right in their own back yards. Fallen angels, witches, satanic sacrifice, blood drinking. It was almost too perfect, too easy.

SO SHE'S got her own little coven of blood witches now? Nathalia had never been one to think something through. She had opinions, and strong ones at that, that seemed to shade and color all of her decisions.

"She didn't say that." Maeve had dealt with Nathalia's prejudices long before she had the power to support them. The new Abbess had always wanted to free the Daughters to exercise their powers more fully. That meant letting them use every technique they knew of. As long as no one was being harmed, what could be the damage?

Jolie doesn't interpret her dreams. She trusts us to do that. And I think it means Tara Kay has gone back to her SOFE ways. Nathalia wanted to intervene. She wanted to go to the former Daughter and tear apart her gruesome coven before they accidentally killed someone.

Jolie spoke up. "There was a lot of blood." She stifled a yawn, triggering the same in Maeve. It was late for the two mothers. Eleven p.m. used to be when they got ready to go out. Tonight, Jolie had already been asleep and dreaming before the clock hit that. That's what having young ones did. "But it wasn't like the premonitions I had about the SOFE. Those were scary. Dark. This one wasn't evil."

"Tell us again. What exactly was she doing?" Maeve got her pad and pen ready. Libby wasn't there so it was up to the Abbess to record the dream. Libby could add it to Jolie's achievement book tomorrow.

"She wasn't really doing anything." Jolie closed her eyes. She always did when she was trying to remember a dream exactly. "She's naked, bleeding. Everyone is."

Everyone is naked or everyone is bleeding?

Maeve shot Nathalia a look that said "stop interrupting."

"Both. They're outside. It's night, but I get the feeling this ceremony has been going on for a while. Maybe it started in the day, I don't know." Jolie looked at Maeve. "I'm sorry. I shouldn't be talking about maybes. Let me start again." She closed her eyes again and only started her recap after a deep cleansing breath. "We're outside. It's dark but I can see perfectly fine. I'm naked. The people around me are naked. Men and women press against me. I'm aware that there's never been a gathering like this before. Then I see her. She's the one we've been waiting to see.

"Kay's got her usual green hair and she's standing in front of a giant tree, her feet buried in ankle deep soil. She's flanked by two of the most gorgeous people I've ever seen. They're two extreme versions of the same beauty. He is dark skinned with long black hair. Wild and hard, he's the opposite of the woman on Kay's other side. She's fair skinned with hair so light it's almost white. She's curled and pressed and groomed. Pampered, a Marilyn Monroe type, she looks soft. All curves, she contrasts with his angles.

"We all inch forward, waiting our turn for an audience. We pour out some blood on her. Then we wait as it runs down her body to the ground. She watches us make our offering and then closes her eyes. She listens. When she opens them, she either opens her arms and takes us into her embrace or she doesn't. To be rejected is devastating. When it's all over she speaks to us. She's covered in blood but she's so happy. She's proud of us. She climbs the tree." Jolie shrugged. "That's it." She rubbed her eyes with her fists, like a child boohooing.

"Go home, Jolie. We'll talk more tomorrow."

Jolie stood and stretched. "Tea?" she asked. Jolie and Maeve had been having morning tea together since they were pregnant. It was special brewed to settle their morning sickness, but the medicinal ritual had become an occasion that they both enjoyed. Now, while they visited, their daughters could play in the morning sun when no one else but toddlers and their mothers were awake.

"A'course. Thank you for bringing this to us right away." Maeve knew Jolie could have waited to tell her about her dream over morning tea. Instead, she'd gotten out of bed.

Jolie made a dismissive "it's nothing" wave of her hand, yawned and left.

SATURDAY NIGHT was slow at Bare A$$ets. Really slow. Lowest attendance Kay had ever seen. The difference was the people outside. It had been a long time since the club had protesters. Sure, they were a regular at Merv's, the Calum movie rental store that carried pornography. They didn't have to be very creative with their picket signs when the business name rhymed with perv's. But Merv's was right in town, a good place to picket. Bare A$$ets was out on the county line; nobody to see or document their efforts.

Their objections didn't really do anything to Merv's business. People were going to rent videos and there wasn't anywhere else to go. People outside couldn't see what they were renting. It was more to annoy Merv into changing his store. It didn't work. Out here it was working. There was no "I'm just renting a rom-com" to hide behind. If you went into Bare A$$ets, everyone knew what you were there for.

The few men who did come through the line had their spending enthusiasm greatly reduced by the experience. Some were regulars who hated all things religious, and a few were new faces. No one was certain those unknown faces weren't plants by the protesters outside. The sheriff's office didn't make their usual token appearance. When Crash had called them about the protesters, who were technically breaking the law by being so close to his place of business, he was told that everyone was out on patrol. Dispatch had said that they had better things to do than help a pimp who employed satanic witches.

She'd hung up on him.

Then Crash had given every customer a free lap dance with the girl of their choice. Not a single one had picked Kay. Hurrit was her only paying customer.

As she danced for Hurrit, Billy and Oren sat apart. No one had approached them all night, not common in a place where the money was made through solicitations and alcohol. Billy guessed that Sarrum Arakiel was using that camouflage he'd told them about. He wondered if anyone could see them at all. He was about to ask when he realized someone could see them. Kay hadn't taken her eyes off of Sarrum. She did a move that put her pussy particularly close to Hurrit's face and the vitala's eyes went solid black.

"I don't know how you do it. I grew up in a pretty promiscuous and limit free environment…"

"With the Daughters of Women." Sarrum Arakiel's voice was crazy seductive and almost alien. It was hard to pinpoint exactly what was different about it, but it was off.

"Yeah. I lived with them in Austin, and I was exposed to every flavor of sexual appetite. My parents had other people in their bed. They swapped and all that but I'm not sure I could do it. I want my partner to be mine, you know?" He had slept with plenty of the women on the compound, but they never took him seriously. He was always just a casual partner. He had grown up there and those women would always see him as that little boy who loved the garden. Thinking of home made his heart ache. He needed to get back there. He was hoping that with Maeve's magic at work for him, he would finally have what he'd always wanted: a genuine and passionate monogamous relationship. He had yet to see her, so the recognition spell hadn't been triggered yet. He was beginning to doubt Maeve's abilities. He was probably the first one to do so. Dubious was not a word that was used to describe her rare and amazingly powerful talent.

"No, I am sorry. I do not. I thought the days of owning one's spouse were gone."

Billy protested, "They are. That's not what I mean. I just want to be the only one she wants to be with and I want to only be with her. Don't you want that with Special K?" Sarrum Arakiel didn't say anything further so Billy plowed forward, convinced he had offended the Nephilim. "It's fine for other people to do what makes them happy but I can't share my wife."

"Sarrum Sinnis TaRaKay is not my wife."

"No, I know, Sarrum."

"Call me Oren. It is the name she has given me; therefore, I am Oren."

"I know she's not your wife, Oren, but she's your Sinnis. Hurrit said it meant she's your woman, your spouse."

Oren shook his head. "Not *my* woman. She is *the* woman of the Arakiel family line. She is not destined to be mine: *I* am for her. Whatever she desires I will provide, no matter what the cost to myself or my children. Their lives were only to ensure hers. She lives. Their duty is fulfilled. My children's lives can be ended if it would serve her." Oren looked at Billy squarely. Billy recoiled at the flames he saw there in the Nephilim's eyes. "You would do fucking well to remember that, young one."

"Stop trying to scare my friend." Tara Kay had heard the whole exchange. She was equal parts relieved and disappointed. No, she didn't want any man to think he owned her, but a little jealousy on Oren's part would have been appreciated. She wanted him to feel possessive about her. She held out her hand to Billy, pulling him to stand by her when he took it. "No one's death will ever serve me. Come on. Party's over. Crash is closing up early and sending us all home. You can ride with me and Hurrit. Oren can find his own way home." Oren had yet to set foot in an automobile, hers or anyone else's. She honestly didn't know how he got around. "You're coming too, Melody," she called out over her shoulder.

Kay pulled Billy back into the dressing room with her. Crash was in too foul a mood to fight her on any breech in etiquette. She slid her rainbow dress on over her head, grabbed her bag and she was ready to go. Melody wasn't far behind and with her came Hurrit. He strode across the room to the exterior exit and without preamble, opened it for Oren who stood in door jam, leaning on one massive shoulder. Sound poured in from the parking lot.

"Natives are getting restless." Melody blanched as soon as the words were out of her mouth. Her eyes when to Hurrit. "I'm sorry. I… It's just a saying. I'm sorry."

Hurrit wrapped his arm around her shoulders and pulled her close. He whispered to her and put a kiss on her dandelion hair. "We do need to go, though. Ready, Sarrum Sinnis Tara Kay?"

"Yes. Let's get the fuck out of here. And it's just plain Kay."

"There is nothing plain about you, my queen."

She was about to protest but the wave of hateful yelling washed over her. Oren swept her under his arm and Billy took her hand on the other side. They were shielding her from seeing the protesters, but they couldn't keep her from hearing. They weren't just shouting the regular stuff. She was shocked to hear that it was directed at her specifically.

"Go back to Austin, weirdo!"

"We burn witches in Calum."

"Devil worshiper!"

"Satan's slut!"

"God will drive out the demons and their women."

Melody hissed and Hurrit growled at the crowd.

Oren made a wall between her and the hate when they got to her car. Billy slipped behind the driver's seat and into the back seat. He pulled the front seat back into place and Kay quickly got in. Melody was in the passenger seat and Hurrit was behind her. Oren leaned in and kissed Kay in that way that made her knees weak and her brain go to mush.

He spoke over her shoulder to Hurrit, "I will make sure none follow and will meet you there."

Kay pulled out of the lot quickly, kicking up gravel onto the protesters. "What the hell's got them so riled up? Club's been there for-fucking-ever."

"Hate like that is usually caused by Akhkharu in the area. Their presence causes a spike in violence wherever they take up residence. They feed off of it. And there's the vrykolak that attacked Billy. Those never get too far from their makers. The problem with that theory is that Nephilim can sense their brother betrayers and Sarrum Arakiel cannot find trace of one."

Only a few seconds away from the county line and its row of brightly lit liquor stores and titty-bars and the darkness was absolute. The headlights cut a path through it along the winding blacktop but beyond that the trees blocked all natural nighttime light. Even the near full moon couldn't penetrate the canopy over Rural Route 4.

"He wants to be called Oren. He told me tonight. Again," Billy said softly.

"That may be so, but he is my elder. There are so few of those in this world and I prefer to use the formal with my king."

Kay turned her attention from the road when Melody let out a soft sob. "What is it, Aunt Melody?"

Melody turned in her seat, bending her knee and folding it under her. She wiped her eyes with the back of her hand. "I'm so unworthy."

"What! Don't let those fuckers get in your head. They wouldn't know godliness if it bit them in the ass."

"It's not them. It's just that there are so many who have carried the burden for so much longer than me. They have spent hundreds, sometimes even thousands, of years protecting their assigned family, their portion of the bloodline, just waiting for you to be born and then you're born to the youngest of us. I don't deserve to be your guardian."

Kay gaped at Melody.

Hurrit clapped Melody's shoulder over the seat. "Remember when I told you the last time I fed was twenty years ago? Melody was that meal."

Kay swerved. "You said you only feed when the mother calls on you to 'make' another." She looked from the rear view of Hurrit over at Melody. "Fuck me sideways with a barbed cock."

Her aunt looked back at her with solid black eyes and smiled sadly and rather apologetically with the shark teeth-filled mouth of a vitala.

They drove the rest of the way in silence. Kay screeched to a halt in front of the stone home. "Boys, could you give us a minute alone." It wasn't a question. Their exit was awkward since there were only two doors and the guys were in the backseat. Kay closed her door and waited for Melody to do the same. "Why didn't you tell me?"

"What? That I was a vampire?" She had that same lisp that Kay had come to recognize. It was because of the extra row of pointy teeth. "That I was 'made' by a six-thousand-year-old vamp for the sole purpose of looking after and protecting you? That when you came in after awakening Sar...Oren, I could hardly contain my hunger? I had to leave right after that because my hunger mask was so blatant. That even now it is hard to think of anything except how delicious your blood would taste? Do you honestly think any of that would have gone over well?"

"No, I guess not."

"You didn't even know what you were when you came into the club on Thursday. I did the only thing I could: I called Hurrit. He had heard the mother's voice that morning telling him to go to his maker, but he didn't even know where Oren had gone to ground. When I called it was the sign he'd been waiting on. He came immediately."

Kay laughed. "I didn't think he was the type." Melody didn't get her joke or maybe her mind was just focused on more serious matters. Billy and Hurrit lapped the car and soon Oren joined them. They spread out, circling, always circling. "Tell me about the beginning."

NINE

Melody had met Hurrit when she was twenty-four and living in Oklahoma. It was the late 1980s and she was doing the same that she did now, stripping. She made plenty of money at it and she planned to make as much money as she could while her looks held out. Hurrit had come into the club where she worked. He was gorgeous.

She pursued him and he resisted for a while. They dated. They moved in together. She tried to get pregnant "by accident" and when she confronted him about it, he told her. He couldn't get her pregnant because he was a vampire. She hadn't believed him at first, of course. She had never seen him drink blood, but she had seen him put away a cheeseburger or two. He told her that he only drank when he turned another. Melody tried to force his hand. She had asked him to turn her because what drawback was there if a vampire could walk in the sun, not murder, and still eat food. He said no. He only turned those who were called by the great mother.

Then one night while they made love, Ki had spoken to Hurrit, telling him that Melody was chosen. Melody saw his hunger mask for the first time. He had drank her blood and given her his. It was while his blood flowed down her throat that Melody had heard the mother's voice for the first time. There was a family who needed a guardian and Melody would be that for them.

After the change, Hurrit had cared for and trained Melody. When she heard the mother's voice again it was urgent. The children of that family had been scattered and the one remaining was suffering. That one had almost killed herself in an offering to Ki and Ki had answered with food and protection. Melody left Hurrit to find each of the children, especially the one who had been left behind.

Melody had cared for all the children, but she loved Special Kay. She'd watched over the girl from a distance, interfering only when Kay's life was in danger. When Kay was grown, she'd introduced herself to Kay. Kay knew the rest.

Melody had never heard the mothers voice again, until earlier today. She'd heard the same message that Hurrit had when he drank Kay's blood. It had woken her up and she hadn't been able to sleep since. She was obsessed with the need to come see Kay. See her and drink her blood.

"Here." Kay offered Melody her arm, wrist up. "Go ahead. I offer it freely, or whatever the fuck it is I'm supposed to say."

Melody looked at the pulse, so close to the surface for a second. She may have even licked her lips, before pushing it away. "Not now. Not yet. The mother said we should all come to you together. Plus, I know what the bloodlust is like." Melody knew that Kay wasn't into sex with women. Kay didn't judge lesbians; she just wasn't one. She wasn't even bi-curious. "I can wait until you can separate it from regular lust." Melody paused, as if letting herself come to terms with having to wait.

Kay didn't get into what Hurrit had told her. To him, and she suspected all of his kind, blood and sex were the same thing. "Thanks. Come on. The boys are bored."

They got out of the car and Kay took a moment to enjoy the night. This was why she lived in this horrible little town of East Texas. Early June had the most beautiful nights. Too early in the season to get up to triple digit temperatures; as soon as the sun set it was perfect porch weather. It reminded her of all the nights she'd spent swinging from or climbing in her tree.

She smiled at Oren. He had done so much for her sad childhood, just sitting there. Her tree had been so huge that he connected the ground to the sky, like he connected the harsh reality of her life to her dreams of happiness. She had always thought the family land had held her here, but it was him. Deep down, she had known that the tree was more than just a tree. He may have grown there for thousands of years before she was born, but he was for her.

It was early morning and dew had already started to collect on the grass. Tara Kay crossed the distance between them and leaped into Oren's arms, her feet barely wet. She wrapped her arms around his neck and buried her head in his neck. He only needed one arm to support her light weight. Her feet dangled above his knees.

He had also created an army of guardians to protect the bloodline so she could be born. He'd given her Aunt Melody in a roundabout way. Kiyahwe had chosen Melody for her and used Oren's child Hurrit to bring her to Kay. Tara Kay sighed into Oren's neck. She sensed, rather than felt, a fluttering there. She lifted her head to look.

Oren's skin was covered in the vine tattoos but unlike during the heat of the day, the morning glory flowers were opened. The leaves were twisted into tiny tight tubes. The bloom closest to her face had shrunk for a minute because of the warmth of her breath and was now spreading back out. She stroked its violet petal and wondered if she imagined the skin was softer there than the surrounding. There was no limit to Oren's power, it seemed, so why would a living moving tattoo be any big thing to him. She didn't wonder how but she did wonder, "Why?"

"I am more plant than animal. The leaves, like my hair, contain chlorophyll that allow me to more effectively harness the power of the sun. Nephilim all do this somewhat, using Ud's light to help them absorb nutrients from Ki's flesh, but I learned a lot in my years as a tree. When I reformed my body, I adjusted my major systems so that I breathe in carbon dioxide, soak up water from the air around me, convert sunlight into energy and, like all plants, my waste product is oxygen."

Kay lay her head down on his shoulder with her face out. The flowers fragrance was light and clean but masculine, Oren's own scent. She loved it. It mixed well with her own woodsy pine smelling perfume, which she realized she hadn't used since meeting Oren. She could still smell it though. "That's really fucking cool, but I meant, why do they move and change, not why do you have them."

"The leaves are hardy and can take the full sun, but the flowers are adapted to be more sensitive. They absorb the reflected light of our sister, Annu."

The moon. Tara Kay could see it just above the horizon. Still near full, it would set at sunrise, rising and staying up later as it waned away. So the moon was her sister. Pretty fucking cool. She sent up a little prayer, thanking Annu for bringing the light into the night. Kay couldn't hear Annu like she could hear Kiyahwe, but she got a feeling from the celestial body nearest to the earth.

Oren whispered into her hair, "Your child would like to run in his new form. Annu's pull is strong on him."

Kay turned her body so that her shoulder pressed against Oren's and she sat on his bent arm, her feet now swinging at his hips. She should have felt foolish being carried like a toddler, but she didn't. It felt natural, like sitting on the branch up high in her tree.

She looked at Billy who stood between Melody and Hurrit. They were obviously quite taken by the sight of their Nephilim and Sinnis but were trying to give the two relative privacy for their soft conversation. Knowing everyone there had super hearing and had heard Oren, Kay called out, "So what's fucking keeping you?"

Billy was scratching his arm with one hand and rubbing his ear on his shoulder. He had more than one itch. "Hurrit says I need to wait for your permission before I run off into the woods."

Hurrit spoke up, knowing she knew little about the bond between maker and progeny, "He is indentured to you, bound to execute your will until the time that you release him. He can feed you and feed from only you."

Boyish Billy came back in a flash. "I think he's worried for the tiny woodland creatures I might kill."

Kay snorted. "Billy couldn't hurt a little furry. He's a vegetarian."

"His beast is not. Your friend is a vrykolak, however special in that category he might be, and they must hunt." Oren spoke so close to her face that she imagined she could taste the extra oxygen. Her head felt light, and euphoria tingled her skin. It felt like a light ecstasy roll. Maybe she wasn't imagining it.

"The wolf isn't different from me. I'm still me in the other shape. It doesn't eat meat any more than I do." Billy couldn't understand why everyone was so nervous about him. He was no monster. Of course, he'd never met another werewolf, so maybe he wasn't the normal breed. Wait, he had met one. Well, he hadn't really met it, he was too busy being killed by it. That thing was still out there. He felt like maybe it was his job to find it and keep it from hurting and killing anyone else. He wasn't sure he could kill a living creature, even one so dangerously evil.

Kay's voice broke him out of his worries. "Show me your wolf. I wanna see your magic." She had always loved Billy. His carefree, lighthearted manner was fun to be around. He was good in the sack, too, but it was not to her taste. He was lighthearted in the bedroom, too, and Kay needed a little more passion and less play.

He grinned and for a moment Kay thought of the boy she'd seen in Libby's photo albums. "I'll show you mine if you show me yours." He wanted her to test his theory that Oren's blood had healed her shredded ability.

Kay hopped down and shrugged. "You first." Her bond with Billy was strong but it was changed. She no longer wanted to have sex with him. She wanted him to drink her blood. Maybe it was the maker bond, but maybe not. She felt the same about Melody and was beginning to suspect her attraction to Hurrit wasn't sexual at all.

Billy took off his clothes and handed them to Melody. She folded first the shirt and then the pants and boxers and put them on the car. His shoes went beside his pile of clothes on the hood. He rolled his shoulders and neck, kicking out his legs and shaking out his arms. He was thin and very tall with the tan to match his gardening obsession. He sometimes joked that the sun was forcing his hair and skin to the same shade of brown but did it by lightening one while darkening the other.

The rest of him, no matter how tall he grew, would never catch up to his hands, feet, and ears. His face was pleasant with an easy smile and brown eyes that sparkled and was framed by perpetually messy "devil-may-care" light brown hair. His eyes, nose, mouth, and ears were all extra-large, giving him a somewhat adolescent appearance, like he hadn't grown into them yet. She wanted to say something about "all the better to see, smell, hear and taste her with."

He turned his face up to the moon and closed his eyes. Billy began to shake. Then he started to convulse. His head whipped this way and that, like he was trying stretch his neck further than was possible. His bones made a snapping noise and Kay gasped. His knees bent back in the wrong direction and he dropped to all fours. His bones and muscles were changing. He grew in both mass and density. The bones of his face shattered and reformed in a muzzle. Hair tore through his skin. When it was finished and he stood on all four lion-like paws, he panted.

"Holy shit, Billy. That must have fucking hurt. Are you okay?"

Hurrit answered for him, "The change does hurt but it will lessen as he learns to make it happen faster. He already shaved off half the time of the first change. You made him strong, my queen, much more able than any I've known."

"Have you ever made a were?" Kay asked but her eyes were locked onto Billy. He seemed to be recovering quickly. He shook his fur in that doggy way that started at the neck and went down the spine to the tip of the tail. Everyone but Kay jumped at the movement. She shot Hurrit a look when he tried to step between her and the vrykolak.

"No, my blood can only duplicate my form. I make only vitala. My blood is not pure like Sarrum and Sinnis. Over the years the vitala I make are weaker and need to feed more often. They are completely unable to become makers, so diluted is their blood. Some have even died."

Hurrit had said died, not been killed. Kay tried to imagine what a vampire old enough to die of old age would look like. Her blood was special, even more so than Oren's. Maybe it did more than just banish the hunger. Maybe it could strengthen Hurrit's children and even give them the eternal life that one expected with the title of vampire.

She heard Kiyahwe's voice then. Lightning filled her whole body and Kay could feel the increase in neuronal activity in her brain. It seemed to come up through her toes and up to her mind, as if her feet were the organ of the sense of hearing, instead of her ears. It made sense that she could hear the great mother earth only through direct contact with the ground.

That is precisely what it will do. You are my chosen vessel. The world will live forever more because of your birth. You will give them an awakening. I owe the children of Ki much because of my past attempts to destroy them. Through Ki, I have come to love them as my own children. For I so loved man, that I chose you to carry my blood and my power. So that whosoever drinks from you in righteousness shall not perish but have everlasting life.

If any shall spill your blood, I will rise up to defend you. If you pour your blood out on me, I shall give you your every heart's desire. Much is given to you and much is expected. When the Shinar come to destroy and take life from Ki, you and your children will send them back.

It was the first time Kay had heard Kiyahwe refer to Ki as a separate entity. Everyone else seemed to refer to the earth as Ki, but she had always been Kiyahwe to Kay. She knew something Oren and Hurrit didn't, but she couldn't remember what it was. It would come back to Kay when Kiyahwe felt it was time.

Kay had lost track of her body. She was sinking when awareness came back. She fought off Oren's attempts to hold her. She needed to be down. It was an irrational need to drop no matter what was occurring around her. She had no vision nor hearing nor sense of surroundings. It was a seizure. She'd had them before. It usually coincided with smoking too much pot and holding her breath for too long trying to absorb more THC. Her body would tremor and twitch gently until her senses came back.

"Well, that sucked the high hard one." Kay wasn't sure anyone could understand her yet. Hurrit and Billy were fighting. Physically. "Stop it!" she yelled, and they listened. Both were breathing heavily.

She remembered what had happened while she heard the mother's voice. The communication had been instant: an upload of information that would rival the speed of any computer. It had triggered a seizure and set off a chain reaction. As she fell Oren tried to stop her. Billy, in his were form, had growled at the Nephilim and jumped toward her sinking form. Hurrit had misinterpreted the beast's actions for a threat.

Kay moved her fingers. Billy came forward but everyone was tense. He licked her upturned wrist and palm. When she smiled, the tension broke. Billy moved on to lap at her face and she tried to open her eyes. They were open already, just her vision had gone black. She blinked, trying to focus on anything. The doggy kisses were helping bring her back.

She wrapped one arm around Billy's shaggy neck and pulled him off as she sat up. She buried her face in the soft fur of the brown wolf's shoulder, hiding from the rest of them. Seizures triggered an irrational embarrassment. She didn't want everyone fussing over her, though she knew there wasn't much chance of avoiding it.

She told them, "It was just a seizure. Billy's seen it before. He was trying to tell you to leave me alone. I don't like to be touched during…"

"How could you not know she was epileptic? You are her guardian!" Hurrit turned on Melody, his worry needing focus.

"She's not. I mean, she wasn't. Her medical records don't say anything about it and she's not on medication." Melody defended herself.

Oren's voice was louder than normal and soothed at the same rate as it inflamed. "First child of Sinnis Tara Kay, you should have shifted back to human form. You should have told us if you had information about the health of your maker."

"Enough!" She hugged Billy tighter. She didn't want him to shift back yet. Then it came to her, what she had to say. "Up," she told Billy. He rose to stand on all fours, lifting her up with him. She stood, resting her weight on his larger frame. "Billy is my progeny. I have not released him from my service. No one is to ever come between us again. He is not capable of hurting me." She met each of their eyes, making sure they understood her command. She took a deep breath. "It's not epilepsy. It happens sometimes as a response to certain drugs. This time Kiyahwe just short circuited my brain. She spoke too fucking fast for me, like I was a high-tech flash drive instead of the old timey typewriter I am." Her speech slowed as she went on. She was tired.

She threw one leg over Billy's back and lay face down in his silky softness. She thought about making a joke about back hair, but she was too tired to formulate it. Billy padded softly inside the stone house. He took her to her room, where she slid off his back and into bed. He left pushing everyone away, out the door.

"Oren. I want Oren." Her voice was barely louder than a whisper, sleep was already taking her.

The door closed and a warm, deliciously hard body slid under the covers beside her. She turned to him, slid her leg between his, tucked her head into his side and went to sleep. Oren may have been singing but it could have been a dream.

"DON'T LOOK at me," were her first words in the morning light. She was embarrassed. Kay didn't want people to know about any weakness in her. She didn't want to feel their pity. She didn't want them to change the way they acted toward her. She was not a weak little waif who needed coddling.

She heard a tearing noise and flipped over to see Oren pull a strip of cloth from the covers. He used it to blindfold himself. He held his hands up in surrender and then tucked his arms, crossed, behind his head. The position highlighted the lines and details of his incredibly muscled arms and chest. A thin trail of almost invisible green-blond hair pointed down under where the quilt covered his hips.

Kay took a minute to look at him. She could have taken a month. Oren was a god. A bronze god. In the daylight the conical flowers were mere purple twists, but the leaves were full. Hunter green, veined in emerald, his tattoos were mesmerizing.

Oren jumped when she touched him. She traced the vines over his stomach, chest, and shoulders. He lifted his head up to free his hands when she tugged on them. He spread them straight out, open to either side, so that she could finish her finger tour of his tats.

She climbed on top of him and planted kisses on every leaf of his left arm, making her way up his neck. When she got to his face, she scraped his lips with her teeth before kissing his mouth. He let it escalate at her speed, not opening his lips until her tongue darted out, requesting admittance. He allowed her to explore his mouth and only when she tugged at his tongue did he return the favor. The kiss heated up and she put her hands on either side of his face. He wrapped his arms around her, and she stopped.

She tisked at him playfully. "Don't touch me either, Oren." She spoke into his mouth and he breathed it in. She reached behind her and unwrapped his arms, pushing them back to their open placement. "I am in control today."

Straddling him and sitting up on her knees, she pressed her warm wet center through her thong to his stomach. She pulled the rainbow dress she'd slept in up over her head. She gripped the hem and pulled. It was easy to tear and soon she had two strips of almost identical length. She tied one of his hands to the headboard bed post, sliding her now nude breasts across the vast expanse of his chest. She had to scoot up and lean further out to secure his other arm, bringing the soft weight of her tits to his face.

Her soft nipple grazed his lip, and he couldn't resist. Oren bent his head forward to take that offering into his mouth. She allowed it mainly because it felt so good. The thing he was doing with his tongue, not to mention his teeth, was sending waves of pleasure over her skin. Only when her plans got cloudy did she pull away from him. He licked his lips and made a whimpering sound that brought a smile to Kay's face. Now that was more like it.

Hooking her foot under the quilt she flipped it off of him. Looking behind her, she could see his cock was pointed straight at the ceiling. She moved down his chest, stopping only when her thong met his dong. The length of it cupped the crack in her ass. She rubbed her clit through the thin strip of her panties on the top of his dick, right at the base where it met his body. While worshiping his flat, manly nipples with her pink mouth, she didn't bring herself to climax, but she could have. When he sensed she was close, he flipped the internal switch and his tool vibrated. She pulled up, disconnecting. She didn't manage to stifle a shuddering sigh of disappointment.

When she stood on the bed, her feet on either side of his hips, he couldn't stand it any longer. "Please, allow me… I need… just a taste. I will bring you such pleasure." He smiled when he felt her adjusting, lifting one foot and then the other, as she removed the only thing between them. "I need your beautifully sweet pussy."

"Just a taste?"

His blindfolded head bobbed. "Please. Sit on my face. I need to taste your prana."

"I know you're new to English, but what part of 'I am in control' do you have a problem understanding?" She didn't wait for him to answer. She crumpled the thong she had just taken off into a tight little ball and stuffed it in his mouth. "Now we can't have any more misunderstandings. You lay there with that filthy gag in your mouth."

She knelt with both knees on his chest. She leaned forward so that she could talk nasty to him softly. "You wanted a taste, well, there it is. I wore that all night. It rubbed against my cunt and asshole while I ground my pussy against total strangers, against Hurrit. It was the only thing between my aching slit and the Billy beast. I wore it all night while I dreamed of getting fucked. All the while you lay right here next to me, wanting me. It has my pre-orgasm juices all over it and I stuffed it right in your mouth. Can you taste how excited I am?"

Oren's only answer was a kind of slurping sound as he extracted every drop of her flavor. He worked his jaw. What he couldn't suck out, he would masticate out.

She turned so that she faced his cock, her knees now in his stomach, her feet on his chest. "What got me so hot and bothered wasn't any of that. It was the thought of doing this." She took his penis in one hand and feathered her fingers of the other on his downy soft sack. She pulled his foreskin down and exposed the broad head now shiny with pre-cum. She licked the glans clean, paying special attention to the slit at the top where the delicious milky fluid pooled.

Once she had tasted it, all thoughts of seduction were gone. She couldn't take all of him into her mouth. She didn't know how to deep throat. She'd never seen a cock this big, much less tried to suck it. She slid her lips over as much as she could and then worked up and down in conjunction with her hands. She pumped and sucked relentlessly, pausing only once to lick around the shaft for lubrication.

Oren's stomach muscles tightened, lifting Kay slightly, signaling that she was close to her payoff. He clenched his buttocks and angled his hips, pushing his cock further into her throat than she planned. When he came, his prana-filled semen sprayed against her throat instead of the flat of her tongue. She wanted more of a taste than she got, but luckily it hit the few taste buds scattered in her throat and back of the tongue. She swallowed down all he had and then licked away any remnant.

Having Oren orgasm in her mouth was the most erotic and satisfying thing she'd ever experienced. She would never want to suck anyone else's dick as long as she lived. He went soft and the shortening pushed a few more drops out. She lapped them up from his pelvis before they could mix with the small amount of curly green-blond hair there. She sucked his flaccid phallus again before releasing him and resting her head on his hip.

Oren made a noise.

Without looking Kay leaned on one knee and stretched the other leg back. She used her monkey toes to reach inside his mouth, grab the soggy makeshift gag and toss it into the waiting laundry basket plant.

"That was... life changing," he said as she used her big toe to push the blindfold up on one side. With their placements, he could see, but he only had a view of her ass.

"It was just a blow job. It wasn't even a very skilled effort. I've done better. I'm sure you've had a helluva lot better."

He said nothing, only made a strangling noise.

"It's not like I think you're a virgin, Oren. You're a grown ass man. Or Nephi..."

Oren interrupted her and it sounded like he just managed to get the words past his disbelief. "It gets better?! Better than that?!"

Kay chuckled. "You know it wasn't anything special on my part. Unless..." She stopped laughing. Oren wasn't laughing. He was serious. From the swell in his stick, he was about to get really serious. "That wasn't your first blow job. Couldn't be. Fucking impossible that a cock that glorious has never been properly sucked."

"It wasn't done. When I came of age. When I had a need, I took a woman into my home. When she was grasping the furs that made my bed and moaning, I took my pleasure in her body. It was cold back then and many times I pushed inside without even removing mine or her skins."

Kay sat up at that. She spun to face him. "It was cold. And you slept on a pile of furs? Are you talking about the dark ages? Living in castles, fighting with swords and... You're shitting me! You came of age in the dark ages? No. Hurrit said you made him six thousand years ago, and you were already thousands of years old."

One second he was bound to the bed and the next his arms were clamped around her. His back was against the headboard and he pressed her boobs into his face. He spoke with his mouth against her, and the sound combined with the feel sent a rush of liquid to her core. "I have never counted my years. I was born before the calendar. I never lived in a castle, and I was born before man mastered bronze or the making of swords. I fought with a flint-tipped spear and was born in a cave."

Kay was stunned. She had a Neanderthal in her bed. Oren was born in the stone age and not just before the discovery of easily malleable copper. He used flint meaning he could be anywhere from 15,000 to 2.5 million years old. She had just sucked a possibly million-year-old cock for the first time. Kay didn't even date guys more than ten years older than her. Talk about a mind fuck. She laughed until it turned to a moan. Oren was slowly pressing her down against his humming cock. "But....after that...surely...some woman..."

"By then, I had seen what my blood could do. I was uncertain what ingesting my prana from the other source would do to a woman. Others may have tried it. I did not." Oren, in total control, shifted so that his dick pointed up, his tip poised at Kay's entrance. He pushed her down, slowly shafting her. "This. Was. Enough. For. Me." At the last word, he plunged the rest of the way into her.

Kay cried out when his velvet-wrapped stone column hit her cervix and slid past. The tip bent forward, angling just right to press against her A-spot. The shaft swelled in the middle to increase pressure on her G-spot. He moved her in a circular motion never pulling free. The climb was intense, and Kay wasn't sure she would survive the fall.

"Talk dirty to me," she commanded him.

She didn't realize her mouth was open until he licked the inside of it. He spoke into her silent screams. "It was enough. Until I knew the joys of this precious mouth. So hot. So tight. So wet. The clamp of your esophagus around me was exquisite. I will want to feel it again and soon. I am glad you enjoy it because I'm not sure I could refrain from taking you that way even if you begged me. The things I will do to your sweet body will make you doubt my inexperience. The terrible pleasures I will enact on you have not even been fucking invented yet."

She screamed. She didn't know what she said. Maybe his name. Maybe gibberish. She had two orgasms simultaneously, both of varieties she'd never experienced. Time stopped and as her body shattered, her mind soared. She knew every creature who had ever walked the mother's skin or grown in her flesh. She knew the number of humans she would save from death. She felt each penetration Oren would give her and every puncture the teeth of those children would make in her skin.

She rejoined her flesh to hear a flood of profanities pour from her mouth. She clamped her lips closed and enjoyed every tremor and quiver of the wane. When she was spent, Oren laid her on her back between his legs. Her feet twitched on either side of his hips. He was still inside her with no signs of exiting.

"Did I do that right?"

"Wha...?"

"The dirty talking...I have never done it before. The women in my past were more animal than artist and there was not much talk. I want to do what pleases you. I must."

She flung her hands up over her head to hang off the foot of the bed. "You did great. I would have thought you had done it a million times. Did you like it...talking nasty to me?"

"Very much. I have already thought of some more things I would like to say for your hearing pleasure." He reached out and flicked her clit, swollen and protruding from its hood.

She jumped and the room tilted. "Did you make the earth move?"

Oren circled her nerve bud with his thumb as his tool powered up inside her. "No, Sinnis, that was you. You let the mother experience something she hasn't in ages: sexual climax. She wants her vessel to scream again in ecstasy and you will if I have any say, many times before the sun sets."

It was going to be a long, luxurious Sunday.

TEN

Charly Boi pulled up in the cursed old car he was being forced to use since he'd hit that deer. He sat staring at Tara Kay's fixed stone home. It looked brand new. She hadn't mentioned renovations to him, but whatever had kept her from her trailer last night was a blessing. He hoped what he had just seen wouldn't upset her too much. He had stayed away to give her some time with her new beau but had come today to visit, and now he had bad news to give her.

He shifted up into park and killed the engine. Three bodies littered the front yard. He panicked for a split second before all three heads raised to investigate his arrival. Jesus, he had thought…never mind. He wouldn't even dignify his fears by naming them. He knew Special Kay wasn't capable of the things the people in town were saying she was doing out here. Although the men that were standing now looked gorgeous enough to be demons. They had been sunning in their boxers, except Oren, who was totally naked.

Charly Boi got out of the car (he refused to acknowledge it as *his* car), and Kay appeared on the porch with the slamming of his door. The two men he didn't recognize moved themselves between him and Kay, but Oren strode right up to him. The giant gathered up the newest arrival in a great big bear hug. Oren didn't seem uncomfortable in the least, giving the gay man a nude hug. Charly Boi tried to keep his eyes above the waistline. "It's good to see you too, Oren." He smiled. "What happened to the clothes I got you?"

Oren shrugged. "Bitch, I'm at home. Who wears clothes at home?" Oren continued when Charly Boi just gaped at him. "Shit, you're the last fucking person I expected to be prudish about male nudity."

The question had been rhetorical; Charly Boi hadn't expected an answer. The last time he saw Oren, the man had barely spoken five words in English. Now he talked in the same filthy way Special Kay did, with the ease of a sailor. Kay bound down the steps and crossed the yard in an instant. She hugged Charly Boi too. Thankfully she was dressed and so was Melody, who had appeared on the porch, but stayed in the shadows. He didn't need to see naked women. She waved, and he waved back.

"Where you been? I expected to see you last night."

He gestured to the car. "I wrecked the ride. God-damned deer. Auntie Bee let me borrow this pile of shit. If I'd known you were having a gorgeous man convention, I would have found a way to come out sooner. I thought I was giving you some alone time with your new man."

"Oh, I'm sorry." Kay gestured to the two men behind her. "This is Hurrit, an old friend of Oren's, and this is Billy. He lived on the compound in Austin with me. Hurrit, Billy, this is my best friend Charly Boi."

"Nice to meet you."

"Pleasure."

He pumped hands with both. "Believe me, the pleasure is all mine." He leaned over and spoke to Kay out of the side of his mouth but made it loud enough for everyone to hear. "Please tell me that one of your friends is in the market for a very flexible strong black man with a big cock."

Kay punched him playfully in the arm. He tried not to flinch. It wasn't sexy to be hurt by a tiny girl's punch but if she was going to keep hitting him so hard, he was going to ask her to stop slugging him in front of anyone. He had a yellowing bruise from last time.

"Straight to the fucking point, as always." She shook her head and pursed her lips at her friend's candor. "Billy's got a spell on him that won't allow him to fuck anyone but his true mate. Hurrit could be bi. I don't know. Come up to the house. I'll get us some tea."

Kay went inside with Melody. Billy and Oren returned to their places in the yard. They weren't finished tanning. Billy didn't look like he could get much darker. Charly Boi wondered if Oren knew what sun did to tattoo ink. The ornate man didn't seem too worried. Hurrit slipped his brown arm under Charly Boi's arm, around his waist and urged him toward the house. His long silky black hair tickled Charly Boi where his sequined wife-beater left his skin exposed.

Hurrit spoke as they walked toward the house. "In my tribe, as with most of that time, a person like you, with the body of a man and the spirit of a woman, would be highly revered. With the best of both genders—men's bodies are strongest, while the spirit of women hold that title— you would have been a holy man, a shaman."

Charly Boi should have been slightly insulted by Hurrit's assumption that gay men had the spirit of a woman, and that there were only two genders, but he recognized the man's compliment for what it was. There was just a cultural difference. He sat in the porch swing and Hurrit sat on the banister in front of him. The Native American perched with an unbelievably straight back, his hair flowing down behind him, framing his form against the light of Sunday afternoon.

He used his bare foot to push the swing back. When it came closer to him on the upswing, Hurrit continued. "I admire anyone with the bravery to live their unconventional life in the open in a place like this. The past few generations have not treated your kind with the respect all humans deserve."

Charly Boi noticed that Hurrit had said "your kind" not "our kind." "So, you're not gay." He said it as a statement.

Hurrit laughed. "I'm not anything that definable. I have had sex with men and women and everything in between during my long life." Charly Boi didn't think Hurrit looked a day over twenty-five, but Native Americans could age better than other races. "My lust is dampened as of late, but when it rages, it lies in other arenas."

Charly Boi had no idea what the man was talking about, but he nodded his head like he understood. Kay came out with two glasses of sweet tea, saving him from having to prove his comprehension. Hurrit stopped the swing with his foot, holding it still as Kay sat beside Charly Boi. When she was settled and had handed over the glass, Hurrit swung his legs over the banister, jumped down, and joined Billy and Oren in the yard.

Charly Boi gulped down his whole glass before turning to Kay. She was smirking at him. "Hot, huh?" She sipped her tea.

"And bothered." He remembered what he came here for, as if Hurrit's distance had unclouded his mind. "You'll never guess who I got a call from last night." He didn't wait for her to guess before telling her. "Israel Lovejoy. Nothing like getting a call from your school crush to upset your Saturday night plans. Especially when he doesn't call about you but your friend."

"He called about me?"

"Well, we talked for a while before he got around to telling me that you're why he called. You haven't been answering your phone or returning their calls. They've been worried about you."

"After over a year they're worried about me?! Yeah right. Fuck them. They want something, don't they?"

"There's this woman…"

"I fucking knew it."

"…and she's really sick."

"So sick that Camilla can't heal her?"

"Nothing's worked. Ingrid's tried everything. They thought you might be able to grow something."

Kay stewed for a minute. The Daughters didn't care about her. They didn't miss her. They didn't even support her brand of magic. She and her blood magic had been cast out and now they needed her to do what they couldn't. She wanted to call and tell them to go fuck themselves, but this woman would probably die without her help. Tara Kay used her magic to help everyone. It was a personal creed, one that had gone against the wishes of the Daughters' Abbess, Nathalia. No matter how she felt about Nathalia, Kay would do what she could to help a fellow witch. "Fine. I don't even know if my magic works anymore, but I'll try. I need to talk to Ingrid and maybe Camilla first. Did Israel say what she was sick with?"

Charly Boi shook his head.

"I can't tailer make a cure when I don't know the disease. I'll have to get my cell from the trailer. It's gotta be dead. I haven't charged it in six months. Hell, I don't even know where the charger is. At least the trailer isn't too big. Not a whole lot of places it can be."

"That's the other thing I need to talk to you about." Charly Boi bit his full lip and looked Kay in the eyes. "Your trailer's gone."

"Somebody stole that piece of shit?!"

"No. Somebody burned it."

THE TRAILER that had served Kay as her home for so many years was gone. It was burned to the ground. Thankfully this had been a wet year and the fire had put itself out a few feet from the trailer. Anything could have started a fire like this. The wiring probably wasn't up to code. The kitchen appliances used propane. The generator ran on gasoline. But the blackened cross standing in the yard was a giveaway that this fire had not been an accident.

Someone, or maybe a lot of someones, had started this fire, and their message was clear. Tara Kay wasn't wanted in Calum. The people who burned her trailer wanted her gone. She could leave or she could die. Maybe they thought she'd be inside when they torched it.

"Bastards," Melody said, one arm around Kay's shoulders, trying to console her. It reminded Kay that years ago this had happened to Aunt Melody too. When she had taken up with Gerald, a black man, the KKK had burned a cross in his yard. Gerald had moved away, terrified not just because of the Klan but because the crime went completely unnoticed and unpunished. He had begged Melody to come with him. They could start a new life in a new city where no one cared about the difference in the color of their skin. Kay had never understood why Melody hadn't gone with Gerald. Melody loved him, she knew that then, but now Kay knew why her aunt couldn't leave Calum.

She had to stay because of Tara Kay.

Kay turned and hugged Aunt Melody. When she did, Kay felt something tear loose inside and she started to cry. She really sobbed. Melody turned them so that no one else could see her ward. She knew Kay prided herself on staying in control, staying strong. That's what all the language was about. She cursed to fool everyone into thinking she was tough.

Tara Kay didn't know why she was crying. It certainly wasn't over the loss of the trailer. She'd hated that thing. It was a constant reminder of her parents' abandonment. It was a mark of shame, poverty, and failure. She was just overcome with a feeling of sadness for this town, its people, their hate filled lives, and Melody. Mostly her tears were for Aunt Melody.

Kay didn't have much of anything but what she did have had been in that trailer. Her grandparents' wedding picture, with Mamaw in her black dress, because it was the only new dress she had at the time, and Papaw in his navy uniform, was gone. All her baby teeth that she'd kept in a little silk bag because her parents were too strung out to even notice that she'd lost them or remember to play tooth fairy were destroyed. The beaded necklace her oldest sister had made so that she would quit dropping her pacifier was now ash. Kay couldn't remember that or any other sibling's name and now every link she had to them was burned.

Oren watched as his Sinnis cried. He would never let this happen again. He would go into every home of every occupant in this horrible town and remove every memory, every bad feeling of Tara Kay, every desire to see her harmed. He would start with those three boys who chased her on the night she woke him with blood. She would be a goddess in Calum. They would worship her as he did.

"Maybe we should all go to Austin. Maeve will give us a place, I know it. She's in charge now. She doesn't have the same prejudice against men as Nathalia did," Billy suggested. He really wanted to go home. He was going to call his mother as soon as they were done here.

Kay's tears dried. She wasn't going anywhere. This was her family land. Kiyahwe said she needed to be here, her and her army of children, to defend against the coming of the Shinar. No one was going to keep her from doing Kiyahwe's will.

Oren spoke up. "This Nathalia, you say she calls herself by another name now?"

"Yeah, Ereshkigal of the Kafziel family line."

"Then she is reincarnate of Ereshkigal, who will never allow me or my children to live in peace. Her laws forbid their creation. Her hunters killed my progeny after her death. She fears their thirst for blood and sex is a sign of the beast. That is why I started my family here in the new world with Hurrit, where her warriors would not think to go. She cannot know of you, vrykolak, or Sarrum Sinnis TeRAkay's creation, or of Hurrit and his vitala family or she will not rest until you are all dead. She will kill you herself, if given the opportunity."

Hurrit obviously knew of the danger, but Billy and Kay stared at Oren's proclamation. Sure, Nathalia was a bossy bitch sometimes, but she wasn't a killer. Melody stood expressionless. They had all forgotten that Charly Boi wasn't one of them until he yelled, "Somebody wanna tell me what the heck ya'll're talking about?"

THE DECISION was an easy one. It really wasn't a decision. Sarrum Sinnis Tara Kay couldn't live without Charly Boi and Kiyahwe had already given her carte blanch to 'make' all those she deemed fit. Charly Boi didn't really want to be a vampire but who could resist living forever in a youthful body. Hurrit said that if Kay was the one to make the conversion, Charly Boi might never feel the need to drink blood. Without that horror and with being able to walk in the sun, there really was not much of a downside.

Hurrit had taken Charly Boi to Kay's bedroom to be alone. He had been the one to draw from Charly. There had been sex involved. That was apparently very common. If Kay had needed to drain Billy before giving him her blood, they probably would have done it too. Kay was convinced she could give blood without the bloodlust taking over. Hurrit was not as sure but had agreed to play his part and allow her to try. When Kiyahwe had told her it was time, Kay and Oren joined them.

The room was at capacity. Oren hugged the wall as Kay knelt beside the bed where Hurrit and Charly Boi laid. Her friend's breathing was labored, ragged. She could hear how close his heart was to stopping. He looked up at her with eyes that somehow looked both drugged and panicked.

"Help me sit him up, Hurrit."

"He can draw from your wrist, just like Billy did."

Kay shot Hurrit a look that made the six-thousand-year-old vampire lurch into action. He sat up, bringing Charly with him. They sat on the edge of the bed, Hurrit spooning Charly's back, Charly sitting between Hurrit's knees and Kay kneeling between Charly's, facing him.

"Billy was dying and unconscious. Charly is awake and aware and capable of making the decision. He will bite me himself. He will know that he made the decision and that nothing was pushed on him. He will drink from my neck because he deserves nothing less."

Charly Boi was too weak to lift his arms. His Special Kay moved her hair out of the way and leaned her head to one side. All he had to do was let his head fall forward and his mouth was on her neck. He bit down with every drop of strength he had left, doubting he could even break the skin. He didn't taste the first swallow, but it filled him with the power Hurrit had taken from him and more. Charly Boi wrapped his arms around Kay and held her close as he swallowed her blood in gulps.

Kay willed the wound closed and pulled away from Charly, her second child of the light. Hurrit laid them both back down on the bed. Charly Boi was thankfully unconscious for his conversion and would wake a new man. Kay made it through the conversion without begging for release. She didn't have to fuck those who took her blood. She could choose who slated her sexual thirst.

"I need to be alone with my king."

Oren gathered her up into his arms and took her out of the house.

"MATE-SICK? I'VE never heard of it."

Kay talked on the phone while Billy ran with Melody. He was going to tire his beast out before driving to Austin. Kay was sending him with the medicine if she could successfully make it. Miraculously, the generator hadn't been destroyed in the fire. Billy brought it to the house and used it to charge his cell phone. It had all of the compound phone numbers on it. Kay chose to talk to Ingrid.

"If it has to do with matchmaking, can't Maeve do something?…She did? And what happened?…Okay, okay. What have you tried so far?…Did you mix in any of the rose w…Well, what about the pain killing herbs I left you?…No, I'm not coming back. I have a place here, a purpose. I'll see what I can grow. It's about five and a half hours from here. Billy should be there before ten tonight…That's up to him. I think he'll stay for a little while at least. He's really been homesick…I know, Ingrid. I'm sorry it ended that way too…me too. I'll get a new phone soon and I promise to answer it when you call… You too. Bye."

She hit the end button and tossed the cell onto the end table. The mushroom texture couldn't possibly hurt the phone's electronics. Oren spoke softly, "Ereshkigal will kill your vrykolak."

"Fuck Ereshkigal."

Oren smiled. "I believe I said something similar when word of her law reached me."

"Nathalia's not in charge anymore. Billy's the only one who can go." He already had security clearance. They didn't know Melody or Hurrit or Charly Boi. Kay certainly wasn't going back. Not tonight, not ever. "Kiyahwe says it has to be him."

Tara Kay grabbed a needle from the pin cushion she kept in the kitchen. She went outside and Oren followed her. She needed to make an offering. If it worked and the earth answered her, a plant would grow. She couldn't have plants growing willy-nilly in her house, even if it was furnished with mushrooms.

She pricked her finger and a solitary drop landed in the grass. She put the throbbing digit in her mouth. She spoke silently to Kiyahwe, telling her about the woman and what she needed.

Billy came bounding up in wolf form with Melody behind him. His tongue was hanging out of the side of his mouth comically. He stopped a few feet in front of Kay and Melody stopped beside him. She gave the impression of being out of breath but when she spoke it was smooth. "He's damn fast." Vitala didn't really have to breathe.

The Billy beast stretched out, his belly pressed to the ground, his forepaws as far forward as possible and his hind paws back. There was some popping and quick convulsions. Then it was human Billy stretched out on the grass. "And getting faster," Billy said, trying to keep the grimace from his voice.

"I was talking about the running. I've never run with a vrykolak before. Hurrit told me weres existed but I've never met one, only vampires." Melody handed him his clothes which she had stashed on a rock before their run.

"Very quick change, Billy. Your improvement is astounding. You will be flash changing soon and with the slow change goes the pain." Billy beamed at Oren's compliments. The promise that the painful changes were short lived didn't hurt his mood either.

Billy pulled his shorts on so fast Kay didn't even get a glimpse of his junk. He slipped his sneakers on and shoved his socks into his pockets. He didn't bother with the tee shirt, just flipped it over a shoulder. "I'm not sure about leaving you. It seems like a bad time. What, with the cross burning and all."

Kay started to tell him that she could take care of herself, but Oren beat her to it. "The need for you to stay by her side will lessen once she releases you from her service. Sarrum Sinnis TeRAkay is the chosen of the great mother. Ki would not allow her vessel to come to any harm. I am here and my powers are not insignificant. I can move her across the globe in an instant if need be. Plus, she has her three vitala should anything happen to me."

"Two vitala," came Hurrit's voice from the porch. "I don't know what Charly Boi has become." Oren beckoned them with a twitch of his hand. As they came down, Hurrit tried to work it out. "He can't be vrykolak since the full moon didn't shine at his making. He doesn't want my blood so he's not vitala."

Oren wrapped his arm around the progeny in question. Charly Boi made no objection, even melting into the Nephilim's embrace. Oren sniffed his skin and then bit his neck.

"He's insatiable in bed, almost like a…"

"Lilitu," Oren finished Hurrit's sentence as he pulled away from the sampling. He had only taken a drop, but it had enraged Tara Kay and inflamed Charly, who now rubbed against the Nephilim.

"…but it can't be. Maker and progeny must be in love for the conversion to result in a Lilitu." Not just love, but sexual love. Hurrit only had his experience with Oren to pull from.

Charly Boi continued to act like a cat in heat and Oren allowed it. He even petted the new Lilitu.

"Hands off. Seriously Charly Boi. You know I love you, but I will tear your head off if you touch my Oren again." Hurrit rushed forward, grasped Charly Boi by his shoulders, and pulled him back. Charly was still high in the throes of the bloodlust. He couldn't take the threat as seriously as Kay intended it. She had said it jokingly but halfway through the sentence she realized it was the truth. She turned on Oren. "And you! Don't you ever drink from anyone but me. That's my rule. Fuck-all good your powers will do you if you break it."

Oren tipped his head and bowed to her, as if it was perfectly reasonable that she set rules and threaten him if he should break them.

Kay thought about the way having someone drink from her felt. She wasn't ready to have Oren feel that way about anyone else. "And another thing, no one draws from Oren except me. His 'making' days are over."

Another bow from Oren was followed by agreement from the others. Something in her voice told them she was deadly serious. That something was mirrored in the way Oren looked at each of them. Billy shrugged. He'd been unconscious the only time he'd taken blood and he'd never let anyone drink from him. He didn't really know what all the fuss was about.

"Look!" Melody shouted.

There, at Tara Kay's feet a plant was growing at an alarming rate. Very quickly it went from a bare stalk, to having a handful of branches each tipped with its own flower. The petals fell off, leaving a small white lump that grew in length. The plant stopped growing when it held six cylinders. Kay quickly harvested them and when the last was plucked, the plant retreated back into the ground.

"I guess that answers the question of my abilities. Here Billy. Break this under the sick woman's nose and when she wakes, she'll be on her way to recovery." She placed one pod in his hand.

Billy looked at it. "That's it?"

"That's it." Kay put the others in his hand. "You better take all of them, just in case they're easily snapped. Don't want you driving all the way there, just to have to turn back around."

Billy gave her a quick kiss on the cheek. "Speaking of driving all that way, just where can I rent a car around here."

The thought that there was a Hertz around here was laughable. "You can take my car." When Billy just stood there, she added, "Keys are in the ignition. Oh, shit, sorry I forgot." She used her most official sounding voice to say, "I, Sarrum Sinnis Tara Kay Woods of the Arakiel family line, do release you, vrykolak Billy Barnet, my first progeny, from my service."

There was no great thunderclap but Billy and Kay both felt the shift. Billy needed to go to Austin and, for the first time since the attack that had almost cost him his life, he could go. He was able to leave his maker. He didn't even feel sick about it. Billy took all three porch steps in one and disappeared inside. He came back out with his hiking pack. He was tucking his cell in his pocket. His mind was clearly on something else because he got into the yellow Chevette, started it, and drove off without another word.

ELEVEN

Billy didn't stop for anything other than gas. He was desperate to get home, specifically to his own room and his own bed. He felt sick all the way home, like he had eaten something rotten. Worse than that, it felt like he had done something rotten and was waiting for it to blow up in his face. He drove that car hard, speeding the whole way. It came to a shuddering stop and he barely had it in park before he was out. He left the door open. He didn't turn off the engine. It died with a loud clang.

He parked on the side closest to the library and his family's quarters. He didn't go through the front entrance. He didn't stop to check into the Abbess' office. He didn't go straight to the medical wing where they no doubt had this very sick woman he had made this trip to bring medicine to. He went straight in the library entrance. He didn't acknowledge his mother when she called to him. He went through their living room, down the small hall and into his room.

His heart skipped a beat.

In his bed lay his mate. He recognized her as such immediately. She was why he had needed to get home so urgently. She was the sick woman. She had mate sickness and it was his fault. He had left to hitch-hike across the country taking away her ability to follow the call spell and come to him.

He knelt by her. He took the pods from his pocket and broke one immediately. He waived it under her nose. Her eyes fluttered. They opened for a second, flashing with recognition, before closing again.

"Oh, Billy," she whispered.

"It's me. I'm here." He broke another under her nose. "I'm so sorry it took me so long. I'm so sorry…" He paused.

"Minali," his mother's voice came from behind him. "Her name's Minali."

Minali's eyes opened again. "I am so sorry, Minali. I will spend the rest of my life making it up to you, just please don't die. I'm here and I'll never leave you alone again." She smiled weakly at him before shutting her eyes again, as if they were too heavy to hold open. Billy noticed the gap between her front teeth. He had always loved that in a woman's smile. He broke another cylinder but before he could put it under her nose someone snatched it away.

Smelling salts! That's the miracle we've been waiting on? Smelling salts? Nathalia's voice filled his mind even as her body filled the room.

"Billy's her mate. It isn't the medicine that matters. Tara Kay sent just what Minali needed, him." Libby's voice was calm.

Billy didn't hear it. He didn't decide to change, either. It just happened. Boom. He was a growling wolf, so very out of place in the tiny bedroom. He was glad Minali was asleep. He thought this might be something that he should break to her gently. There was nothing gentle in him now. Nathalia had barged into the room where his unclaimed mate had almost died. Her voice, her stance, her very presence was a threat to Minali and to top that off she was speaking ill of the work of Billy's maker. This was escalating quickly.

Vrykolak? Abomination!

Libby's quick thinking saved them all. She pulled Nathalia out the door, slamming it closed behind her. She spoke softly through the door. "Billy, no one is threatening your mate. We need to talk to you, to understand what's happened."

They did not see Billy flash change back into his human form. His first change had destroyed his clothes. He didn't bother with replacing them. He crawled into the twin sized bed beside Minali, gently scooting her body toward the wall so that he could put himself between her and the door. Careful of the iv, he slipped his arm under her head and cradled her too frail frame against him. Her breathing already seemed less labored to him. She muttered his name in her sleep.

Nathalia needed to be in the same room with a person to talk to them even less than a vocal speaker. She spoke to Billy quietly but in a way that he could not ignore. *Tell me what Akhkharu has done this before I end you. I will kill the breaker of Ereshkigal's Law to give you peace, but I cannot allow you to hurt that girl.*

"Hurt her? Why would I hurt my own mate?" he whispered, knowing she could hear him. "The only person I want to hurt right now is you if you threaten my maker again. I wasn't made by an Akhkharu. I'm a child of the light. Oren said you wouldn't understand."

Oren? Nathalia wondered. There was no Nephilim by that name. She had never known a vrykolak of the light. They were all vicious creatures, hungry for gore and violence. Who would create such a progeny? As soon as she asked herself the question, she had her answer. Only one Nephilim had ever flaunted her laws so flagrantly. The Oldest was in league with Tara Kay, the blood witch.

Eiran appeared behind Nathalia. He wrapped his arms around her. They dissolved, moving through the mother earth cell by cell. She didn't need to tell him where they were going. He knew. He would reform them prepared for battle.

"THEY ARE and have always been. They did not make life but are made of life. They are one and they are many. They are called by many names but take none as their own. To name is to limit. To name is to detach, dividing life and power, making it the sole property of the named. Those Who See and Observe have no beginning and no end. They have no birth nor death, no children nor parents.

They send pieces of themselves out to observe where life exists and could grow to become eternal. They wait until the day they can harvest that life.

"But this story is not about them…

"The animals of the blue planet were as varied as they were numerous. They grew and changed over millions of orbits around their star. Many types were lost but each time two more were ready to take their place. 'The One Who Was Sent to See and Observe' grew tired of watching, forgot what to watch for and why. Then a few of the animals began to use tools for more than survival. They made art, expressed their emotions. They were aware of themselves as finite beings. 'The One Who Was Sent to See' took interest in those few, helped them in small ways so that they could continue to survive though they had no natural defenses. 'The One Who Was Sent' saw that they had an ability none other had: the ability to adapt, not just every few hundred generations, but to remember and apply those memories to new situations. They adapted to change itself. To 'The One Who Was' the most remarkable thing of all was that these animals lived in a way none other had. They enjoyed being alive. 'The One Who Was' desired the same.

"After millions more orbits around the star that gave the blue world warmth and light, what 'The One Who' had begun to call Ud, the animals became more than animals. 'The One Who' grew jealous. 'The One Who' wanted more. 'The One Who' took a name and a form. 'The One Who' became the Goddess Yahweh. She severed Her connection to the rest of Her, 'Those Who See and Observe'. She took Her life and power and kept it as Her own, putting up a veil around the blue planet.

"Yahweh grew lonely. She looked with envy at the women of the blue planet and the way they took pleasures from their men and made children with those pleasures. Yahweh birthed for Herself a race of lovers, the Gregori, She called them. She gave them individual names and they were Her equals in all ways but one. Only She could create life within Her body. They gave Her the pleasures to create with but they could not without Her will.

"Yahweh was happy and did not observe the women of the blue planet change. Her lovers, the sons of heaven, looked down and saw that the daughters of men were beautiful. The daughters had the ability to love. The Gregori fell from Her, choosing to live among the animals instead, taking wives from among them. From these unions the Nephilim were born.

"Too late She realized Her mistake. She had made Herself in the image of woman, coveting their ability to make life but in doing so She limited Herself to creating life only with the help of a male. Hers were gone and She could make none to replace them. Yahweh grew angry. She could no longer create life without aid, but She could destroy it.

"And She did. With floods and droughts, fire and ice from above and below, Yahweh destroyed much of humanity but none of Her Gregori would return to Her, nor would their halfbreed children die. She planted Her seeds of destruction within the minds of men through bigotry and religious fervor. She disguised Herself as a male God, giving men the desire to control and limit their women. She hoped they would destroy the beauty that was woman, forcing Gregori back into Her embrace. Superstition and hate swept the world, but the Gregori did not return to Her.

"The Gregori taught their wives many things and then made war with their Creator. When they knew they would never defeat Her but that their actions only endangered those they loved, the Gregori contrived a plan with the blue planet, whom they had named Ki. The Gregori loved Ki and felt they owed all happiness to her. Ki heard their prayers when they spoke from a circle of agreement. Ki promised the Gregori that she would ready the human women for immortality. It would take time. Three hundred and sixty generations it would take to evolve. The Nephilim would live to see the animal race of their mothers, become more.

"With that promise, the Gregori returned to Yahweh. After a great battle, they forced Her to fall with them and trapped Her within Ki, but to keep Her there they gave up their freedom. Their human wives, to whom they had shared their knowledge and power, lived, as did the children of their love. The Nephilim stayed behind. Forever living, they walk the earth waiting."

Her voice was soft, reverent, but more than loud enough for those in attendance. She alone knew the story's ending, which she now shared. "Yahweh had Her Gregori with Her, but they refused to help Yahweh make life. This should have angered Her but being within Ki was soothing. Ki was mother to all life on earth. Ki allowed Yahweh to join with her in all things. They two became One. Together She answers prayers. Together She protects Her children. She is our enemy no longer; She is our Kiyahwe. She will stand with us when Those Who See and Observe, the Shinar, The Shining Ones, return to this world. If we cannot defeat them, they will take all prana unto themselves, rendering Ki a lifeless desert."

Tara Kay finished her story and came back to her senses. She could not remember learning the tale but knew every word by heart. The fog lifted from her mind and she looked around to find herself in the orchard. She was not alone. Her progeny and Oren's were gathered around her. They seemed enraptured by her story, still drunk on the blood exchange.

Nathalia sat nearby in full warrior attire, weeping openly. A stranger knelt behind her and from the way he was touching Nathalia, trying to sooth her, Kay would have guessed they were lovers. Kay had not seen the former Abbess join, so caught up had she been in the scripture sharing. The Mother's words had taken over and everything else faded away. Kay could see that Nathalia was not the same as she had been when Kay had lived under her rule with the Daughters of Women. Nathalia was a Sinnis with a Nephilim of her own, like Tara Kay. She was unsure of what she had said that could upset these magical beings so.

Nathalia stood and the two Sinnis stared at each other. "What do you want?" Kay asked unceremoniously.

I came to speak to the Oldest about his blatant flaunting of Ereshkigal's law.

Hurrit stepped forward and addressed Nathalia directly. "Sarrum Arakiel Maru answers to none. His actions are not questioned for he follows the instructions of the Great Mother. He does not recognize Ereshkigal's Laws."

Nathalia's ego irritated Kay. It always had. She barely heard Hurrit's defense of Oren. She yelled, "Ereshkigal? You mean *your* law. Who the fuck are you, *Nathalia*, to make laws about what we do with our own blood?"

Nathalia didn't acknowledge the vitala that had the audacity to speak. The female warrior's breastplate dissolved at the neckline, revealing a glowing red jewel buried under her skin. Something about it pulled at everyone there, making them feel sick and drained, ready to put the pain of this world behind them. *I am Nathalia Ereshkigal of the Kafziel family line, First Sinnis, one third of the Sister Fates, chosen warrior...* She paused. She was the chosen warrior of the Shinar. The Shinar, she now knew, were her enemy and the enemy of all mankind. She continued, *and Sinnis of Eiran Kafziel Maru and wielder of the DakuAhu. This birthmark makes me a living breathing 'kill-brother' incarnate. Where is your necklace? Your Nephilim, the Oldest, should have claimed you with it, if indeed you are his Sinnis.*

A voice from the tree behind Tara Kay startled Nathalia. She knew it was the voice of a Nephilim before the tree changed into that form. "Cover your birthmark. There are no lives here that need your collection, Ereshkigal."

Nathalia said nothing to the giant winged Nephilim. She couldn't disagree more. Even so, she willed her breastplate back in place, severing her birthmark's connection to every lifeline there. She had come to kill the results breaking her law. The story of Kiyahwe had stunned her but it did nothing to change her goal. They couldn't be allowed to live. They were abominations, corruptions of humanity.

"Sinnis Sarrum TeRAkay Woods of the Kiyahwe family line has no birthmark because I have no birthright to give her."

The Nephilim's words gave Nathalia more questions than answers. *The Kiyahwe family line? What happened to the Arakiel family line? Did you allow the daughters of your mother to pass away or did you kill them yourself? And what have you done with your birthright?*

"I have no birthright. My father did not weep at my birth, as other Gregori did, their solitary tear infused with powers to give to their Sinnis. He was not at my birth. I do not know if he ever knew I existed. He bedded thousands, my mother included.

"She was barely more than animal, ruled by instinct and fear. I never knew her. She did not name me. When her clan leader saw my need for blood, he feared what I was. He commanded my mother to kill me to stay with the clan or suffer banishment with me. It was a wild and ruthless world they lived in. Exclusion from the safety of clan was the quickest path to death. So, I was killed. My mother stripped me of my warm animal skins and bashed my head with a rock. It was an act of mercy; she did not want me to suffer, freezing to death, or worse, being torn apart by a predator. She buried me in a shallow hole and moved on with her clan. I was only a few moons old, but I remember. I, like other offspring of Gregori, have vivid memories long before a human child would be capable of making them."

Oren paused. He took Tara Kay into his arms. She climbed up, like he was still a tree, and whispered how sorry she was. She was clearly disturbed by his tale. He patted and soothed her. "Do not be sad for me. My mother did what she had to do to stay alive. I would have had it no other way. I do not feel betrayed. As I said, she was little more than an animal. Sometimes mothers devour their young in nature if nurturing them is inconvenient or impossible. I do not know what kind of life she had after burying me. Nor do I know how long she lived. I could not track nor protect her daughters, even if I had known that was necessary.

"What my mother did for me that day greatly outweighs any harm she did. She gave me over to the embrace of my true mother, the Great Mother of us all, Ki. Ki did not speak, not in words, not in those first years I spent in her warm flesh. She gave me all I needed. This was long before Yahwe joined with her, long before the other Gregori fell and took wives. Time after time, when I grew weary of living, I came back to Ki and she provided. The more time I spent joined with her, the more clearly she spoke to me.

"Then there was a change. She pushed me up to consciousness, telling me I was no longer alone. More Gregori had bred with human women and the sons of those unions needed leadership. I searched the world for them, finding the highest concentration among the people gathering into the world's first civilizations, in prehistoric Mesopotamia. I grew to love many of those humans, so smart, so cunning, so civilized, and I made my first progeny. Ki told me how to do this. I tried to teach the other Nephilim what they were and how to live without taking human life. I taught them how to absorb energy from the light of Ud and nutrients from contact with Ki.

"Thousands of years passed. Civilizations rose and fell. Religions rose and fell. I heard of the great crimes of my Nephilim brothers who had taken each other's blood into themselves in a bid for more power. The first Akhkharu were terrible and in such great number. I fought alongside Ereshkigal's warriors, those Nephilim who had not tasted brothers' blood. We hunted the Akhkharu, forming the first Justice Circles, allowing Ud's light to reduce them to ash. When none were left, I was told of Ereshkigal's Laws, some of which I had broken dozens of times. My progeny were hunted down and destroyed.

"I went to ground then, intending to never return in Nephilim form. That is when Ki told me the story of my father, Arakiel. Only then, after I had lived for eons, did I learn his name and through him found my own. I was Arakiel Maru, with no individual name of my own.

"Ki told me that my father did not fall from Yahwe. He served Her. Arakiel was the first Gregori. She sent him to earth to learn about human women so that She might be everything they were but more perfectly. He did his job well, but he was a boaster. He told the other Gregori of the pleasures of laying with human women. Their flaws, their frailty, made them attractive. Addictive. He caused their focus to fall to earth and her female inhabitants. Yahwe killed Arakiel in a fit of rage, realizing Her mistake too late. She killed the one loyal Gregori she had left.

"Ki also told me of the promise she had made to the Gregori. She would prepare the human women for immortality, to better match their sons as equals. The Nephilim were to protect their mothers' bloodlines until the time of the Sinnis arrived. She knew I had no bloodline. I also had no will to return to the living or see my progeny killed again. She had me create another family to look over those she would bless with her own gifts, command over the elements: earth, wind, water, and fire. When my surrogate guardians were made, in a place none of Ereshkigal's warrior would find for thousands of years, Ki allowed me to return to her bosom in the form of a tree.

"Here I slept happily. TeRAkay's blood woke me from my slumber. I took her and made her immortal as Ki would have it. TeRAkay gave me a name, the first that is only my own and not a reflection of my father. I am Oren, the Oldest. TeRAkay is Ki's, pardon me, Kiyahwe's vessel. My body and blood belong to her. She would make her own eternal children and I will not see her desires throttled. Ereshkigal, you do not have the power to overcome me, my Sinnis, and our progeny. Your will does not rule here and not one more of my beloved will fall by your hand or order."

Nathalia stiffened. She did not know if the Oldest was right about everything he'd said but he was right about one thing. She had come to tear apart Tara Kay's blood coven, but with these odds, 200:2 that would be impossible to do. She needed her Nephilim warriors. She would call her first justice circle. Eiran tabalu'd them away. As their bodies were broken down molecule by molecule and transported through the earth, Nathalia knew that Tara Kay was right. She spoke to Eiran. *She spoke the truth. Ki whispers to me that She is Kiyahwe. She has changed and now we must also. I was wrong to think Yahweh was still our enemy. She will help us hold the veil and keep the Shinar, Those Who See and Observe, from returning. That does not change the fact that the blood witch, Tara Kay, and the Oldest broke Ereshkigal's Law. The abominations have to die.*

EVERYONE WAS shocked to see Nathalia and her Nephilim disappear. Everyone except Oren, Hurrit, and three others. The three others, Kay knew from before the ceremony, were the other heads of family. Hurrit and his vitala watched the witches given dominion over the earth. There was another vitala family to whom the protection of water witches fell. The vrykolak clan, mostly men, watched over air witches. The Lilitu, all women, had the responsibility of the fire witches. The heads of each were not as old as Hurrit but were made by Oren himself. Hurrit quickly quietened everyone's fears. "That is tabalu, the way of traveling through the mother earth that only Nephilim and their Sinnis enjoy. They have total control over every cell in their bodies and can break them down, reforming them anywhere around the globe."

"I can do that?" Kay asked Oren quietly, privately.

"No, but I can tabalu with you. Would you like to try?"

"Yes. Get me out of here."

"I like it here."

"So do I. I could live here forever, but right now it's a little overpopulated." As long as he agreed to stay too, but she didn't say that. Her family land had always meant a lot to Kay, but she was beginning to wonder if it was because of Oren that she felt so connected. "Take me somewhere else. Somewhere special to you. Somewhere we can be alone. Somewhere you can show me your true form." It was time she knew more about the man she loved.

Oren smiled at her and for a second, she was sure he'd heard her thoughts. "I know just the place. I am sure my little earth witch will love it." Contact was required for tabalu with a Sinnis. He was already holding her, so he got right to breaking them down on a molecular level.

Being pulled through the mother was the single most amazing moment of Tara Kay's life. It was better than any high. It was what she was trying to achieve when she took drugs. It was what her parents had been chasing their whole lives. The separateness dissolved. There was no Tara Kay. This must be what it was like for Yahwe and Ki.

She mourned the loss of that connection when Oren put the boundaries of her skin on her again. It was short lived. The pleasure of being held by Oren overshadowed it. They were alone. Her eyes were closed as she nuzzled him. She wondered where they were when the sun was bright through her eyelids. Then she realized the light was coming from the side where her face was buried in Oren's chest. She had asked to see his true form. She tried to prepare herself before opening her eyes. She didn't want to hurt his feelings by reacting badly.

She was right to have worried.

Oren was frightening. No wonder the tales of angels visiting humans always started with them saying, "Be not afraid." He glowed, just like the rendering of angels in an old family bible. His wings spread out wide, a huge span. She could only see the underside. They weren't feathered though; they were made of flesh, like a bat's. He was huge and hairy. Thick brown hair covered his head, torso, arms, and legs. His skin was dark and leathery. It was still his face though, the one she'd grown accustomed to, that showed over his beard.

He was bigger. Taller and thicker. "My giant Neanderthal. I'm in love with the damn missing link."

Oren wrapped his wings around him. On the outside they were as hairy as the rest of him. He looked like he was wearing furs, like any other caveman. Kay patted his hair-covered cheek. She could only reach it because he was still holding her. "I could do without this, though."

"Truly?" he asked, a tiny quiver in his deep voice.

"Yeah, beards are a real bitch." She kissed him, his mustache coming between their lips. "They get in the way of all kinds of fun things. And they chafe. Why? You attached to yours?" She tugged on it.

His beard disappeared. "No. Not that. Are you truly in love with me?"

"Don't be a fucktard. Of course I am. How could I not be?"

"You were so angry when I showed you that I was your tree. I knew you felt betrayed. I saw your reaction to Hurrit and thought you might...prefer him. He never wronged you. I felt how aroused you became in the kitchen when he fed from you."

"I was just upset because my tree was, well I *thought* my tree was uprooted. It was a fucking shock, is all. And in the kitchen, if I remember correctly, it was your fingers in my cunt. You had me creaming. Not Hurrit." She had been a little confused by the bloodlust at first but now she knew the difference. Having a few hundred vampires, werewolves and succubus drink from a girl could do that.

"In all my lonely years, I only dreamed of serving you. Loving you. Never that you might feel the same. I will spend every minute we have together trying to be worthy of the love of Sarrum Sinnis TeRAkay, vessel of Kiyahwe."

"Don't go all gushy on me, Oren. I'm not that kind of girl," she protested, but his declarations had an effect. She was naked. She was suddenly very aware that Oren was naked. She thought about his true form's bigger size and then all she could think of was his cock. It was probably mammoth. She could smell her own arousal and she knew by the look in Oren's eyes that he could too.

His voice, if possible, dropped an octave. "And what kind of girl are you?" He didn't pause to let her answer. "Are you the type of girl a Neanderthal like me might drag back to his cave? The type that would fight as I pushed my caveman cock into every tight little hole you have or the type that would moan, begging me for more? Would you bend over a stalagmite, spread wide willingly or would I have to tie your wrists to your ankles to get the view I want?"

That was exactly the kind of crude language and dirty talking that made her gush. She felt a rush of liquid, making her inner thighs slick. She threw her head back. He adjusted her so that she sat on his forearms, one leg trapped between it and his body, the other on dangling. He bent his wrist up, sliding his thick fingers along her slippery folds. His other meaty hand covered her stomach before roughly palming a breast.

She loved the feel of his rough "furs" on her soft skin. His dominating demeanor was doing it for her. The thought of him taking her like an animal, fucking her hard and fast, her so wet that he didn't notice when he slipped from pink to stink, primal pleasure so great he didn't stop when she cried out, almost made her come right then. She thought about how her screams and his grunts would echo through the cave. Wait…

She opened her eyes.

Cave? Stalagmite? "Just where did you talu us?"

"Tabalu is the word. It means to take away. This is where I lived as a man. This was my home before I found your land. We are in my cave." Oren set her down. Her feet rested on a very smooth stone.

It was pitch black in there, but Kay could see fairly well now that she knew what she was looking at. Oren walked around, slapping mushrooms along the way. They, like the ones in her home, glowed, triggered by touch. Seemingly sporadically placed, they lit highly decorated areas of walls and formations. Kay moved around studying the drawings of every kind of life. These were masterfully done, designed and executed in such a way that the animals seemed alive. Her movement gave them movement. Out of the corner of her eye she could see a giant cat stalking her in the grass but when she looked directly at the spot, she couldn't see it.

To her right a stampede rushed by, somehow painted on both the wall and the stalagmites. It gave the primitive paintings a three-dimensional quality. To her left a herd of giant antelope grazed, its young so delicately drawn that the stone had a soft fur-like texture. She chose her steps more carefully after twisting her ankle as she moved toward the back of the cave. Here the images were more human, but she couldn't make out what the scene was.

Oren took her hand, pulling her toward a large indentation in the center of the floor. Opening one wing, he laid down, pulling her down beside him on the soft underside of his wing. When she looked at them now, she could see. These were designed to be viewed while laying down in this exact spot. It must have been his bed. As she looked at the erotic images of prehistoric couples in a variety of positions she knew. "This must have gotten you a serious amount of ass. I mean, a caveman with his own porn. Were the ladies lined up to get with you?"

"No woman has ever seen this. Not before today." His voice was as soft as his wing.

Tara Kay looked around. There was no natural entrance, at least none large enough for a person to fit through. The formations said that at least water had a way in and out, but there was no evidence of humans ever having lived here. There wasn't even any evidence that cave bears or mountain lions had made their homes within. There were no bones from animal leavings, no scat.

This place was beautiful, and Oren had created it for her eyes alone. He had spent years here, alone, dreaming about the day he could bring her here. Tara Kay had never been valued, never been cherished and waited for. Today she was a queen, a goddess.

She turned to Oren, leaning on one elbow, and kissed him. He kissed her back, gently, slowly, as if he couldn't believe his fortune, as if he were to move too quickly or aggressively, she might just disappear. They took their time there in the dirt, exploring each other's bodies, memorizing every curve, angle, and reaction. Kay realized there were tears in her eyes when he came inside of her. She cried because it was the first time she'd ever made love.

TWELVE

Minali was well. Billy was slightly better than well. He was healthier than any human had a right to be. He just happened to be able to change into a giant wolf. Everyone was out of danger. Everyone except Tara Kay. Maeve owed it to the ex-Daughter to try and stop Nathalia from destroying her new coven and killing Tara Kay. Nathalia had taken off in that flashy way of hers. Maeve had no way to follow her except old fashioned internal combustion powered car.

Maeve normally drove a fully electric neighborhood electric vehicle, but it had a max speed of fifty-five mph and a range of only seventy-five miles. She needed significantly more than that to get from Austin to Calum, where Tara Kay lived. Maeve had taken one of the other cars the Daughters owned. They were all communal. She'd come alone. No matter what mindset Nathalia was in, she wouldn't hurt Maeve. Maeve couldn't promise that much to anyone else.

She turned off Rural Route 4 onto the driveway Billy said would be there. It wasn't much of a driveway, more of a five-foot-wide place where the grass was short between two dirt wheel grooves. She started to second guess Billy's directions until she passed a blackened patch with a burned cross in front of it. She hadn't believed places where the KKK ruled still existed. Now she knew better.

She was glad it wasn't night. Now that she was past the burn site, the driveway was hard to detect. It would have been impossible in the dark. This part of the drive hadn't been used as much in recent years. She pulled up to some beams laying in the grass that obviously served to mark the parking, though there were no cars here now.

She stared out the front windshield. The beautiful stone house in front of her was nothing like she'd expected. It was hand built but done so well that she doubted the corners and angles were off by even one degree. The roof was odd looking. It could have been natural, peat maybe. It was large, but not sprawling, and looked quite at home where it sat. There was a greenhouse attached to one side and a wide porch stretched across the entire front of the home. No wonder Tara Kay had been homesick for this place. Even something as archaic as the KKK couldn't deter from its beauty and draw.

She got out of the car and winced when it slammed shut. It seemed irreverent to bring the modern world out here to interrupt the house's peace. She approached the house with her hands at her sides, carefully open to show that she was no threat. She didn't know who was there or if they knew who she was. Nathalia had to have gotten there last night and with her attitude, anyone on Tara Kay's side would now be on alert.

She climbed the wooden steps, noting how sturdy they were despite their apparent age. She knocked and when no one answered, she took a peek into the window to her right. Other than some odd choices in furniture, nothing seemed out of the ordinary. She called out but wasn't hopeful that anyone was within earshot. She didn't see any evidence of violence, but she couldn't shake the feeling that she was being watched as she turned back to her car. That feeling wasn't coming from the house, but the woods.

She breathed a sigh of relief when the cop car pulled up and parked beside hers. The eerie voyeur feeling went away. She went down the steps. A short man got out the driver's seat, put on his hat and started to walk toward her with the purpose of a lawman. A tall black man with a military build got out of the passenger side and reached back, opening the rear door to let a young white man out.

Before the sheriff was halfway across the yard, the young man ran up behind him. Without warning he slit the small sheriff's throat. Just like in the movies, for a second nothing happened and then a red line appeared. The blood flowed out all at once. The sheriff dropped to his knees and then fell face down in the grass.

Stunned, Maeve had just stood there staring. Now she moved. She ran back up the steps onto the porch. When the door wouldn't open, she banged on the locked door and yelled for someone, anyone, to let her in.

"No one's home," the young man told her. "Quit that hollerin'. T'aint doin' nobody no good and it's givin' me a headache."

Maeve quit. She put her hands up and called over her shoulder, "I didn't get a good look at either of you. I don't know what's going on here, but I've got nothing to do with it. Just let me go and I promise I won't be any help to anyone coming after you. I'm nobody. Please. I have a baby at home."

She couldn't see the dagger that he held as the black man climbed the steps. "Oh, but something tells me you are somebody. You have everything to do with what's going on here. You might not be an unclaimed Sinnis, but the dagger wants your blood. Wants it even more than Tara Kay's." He unholstered a gun and put a quick shot in her right foot. He grabbed her and threw her over his shoulder, ignoring her cries. "Can't have you running off the first second we turn our backs. Come on. This is no place for the mother of 'The One' to die. But don't worry, the perfect spot isn't far away."

MONTANA STOOD in the center of the orchard clearing, uncertain what to do now. The woman he'd found at Tara Kay's house lay at his feet, dying. The dagger had demanded her blood and it had a way of getting what it wanted. He'd stabbed her with the white dagger three, maybe four, times in the chest. And what a glorious chest it had been. Her curves were extreme, almost grotesque. He was fairly sure he had missed her heart but from the way she was gurgling, he knew he'd hit one of her lungs. He jumped when two Nephilim and their Sinnis appeared in a circle around him. He held the knife out and pulled the dart gun from his waist belt.

He pointed it at the woman warrior who had destroyed his shoulder, and the entire Paion unit he worked with. She was his biggest danger.

She screamed when she saw the dying woman on the ground. Fire raged in her eyes and her right arm flattened and changed into a short sword using the metals in her body. The two Nephilim were quick to follow suit. He had no chance if they attacked all at once. "She's not dead yet. She will be soon though. I might not be able to get all of you but which of you halfbreeds wants to risk the DakuAhu tasting the flesh of your Sinnis?"

He brandished the dagger in Tara Kay's general direction. Tara Kay didn't have to ask her, Kiyahwe just opened up a hole under his feet. It was just a foot in diameter. When she sucked Montana down it, there should have been blood and guts everywhere, but the suction took every drop with him. The dagger went flying. They could deal with it later.

Nathalia and Tara Kay ran to Maeve. Nathalia shoved Kay away. *Don't touch her! This is your fault.*

"That might be true but, I can save her. Billy was much worse off when I gave him my blood."

No. Nathalia clutched Maeve's bloody body to hers. She rocked back and forth on her knees.

"Think about it, Nathalia. She's going to die unless she gets our blood. Be reasonable! Ereshkigal's Laws were made before you knew anything about us, before you knew anything about how good the children of light could be. You can hold on to those ridiculous rules or you can see Maeve live."

It was true that Nathalia had already broken one of Ereshkigal's laws when she drank from Eiran. That law had clearly been a mistake. A Nephilim and Sinnis could drink from one another without becoming Akhkharu. Maybe she was wrong about them all. *I don't know if it is what she would want.*

"Everyone would rather live than die, no matter what the conditions for that life might be. Do it fast or the decision will be made for you." If Maeve died before they could get the conversion started, she would be an animated corpse.

Nathalia found that she couldn't move. Her body was petrified. Tara Kay didn't hesitate. She tore through the thin skin at her wrist, opening a wound that would last long enough. The earth shifted again, and Kay stumbled away from Maeve and Nathalia. Oren caught her, lifting her to her feet.

Lightning filled her whole body and Kay could feel the increased activity in her brain. She heard Kiyahwe's voice, just like before and Tara Kay prayed a seizure wouldn't follow. The great Mother's words came from her mouth, "We would have the Holy Mother of the One saved, made, but it must be done by the First or not at all. She has been your friend, confidant, even lover and now she will be your child."

Nathalia looked terrified. It was her decision. Just her. There was no real decision. Not when it was Maeve. This would change things, but she would have to deal with that when the time came. She and Maeve would face this together.

Nathalia cradled Maeve. She tore through the thin skin of her own wrist, as Tara Kay had done. She put it against Maeve's too pale mouth. She put her own mouth against a hole in Maeve's chest. She drew the blood from Maeve's lungs. As Nathalia fed from Maeve's generous bounty, the matchmaker began to move under her.

She sounded mournful when Nathalia pulled away. Nathalia tore her other wrist and allowed the blood to run into the stab wounds. Maeve was a horrible sight by the time the wounds stopped flowing, but under all that gore, they could tell she was whole.

The great mother, Kiyahwe, spoke to them through Tara Kay. She knew Nathalia was too proud to give up her misguided laws without motivation. She also knew that Nathalia loved Maeve more than Ereshkigal believed in her own infallibility. She used Maeve to ensure Nathalia would never threaten a progeny based solely on their conversion. Each should be judged based on their life and only Kiyahwe could judge. Maeve would be happy in her new form. It meant she and her mate could live forever and see their daughter grow up to save their world and every life on it.

So caught up in hearing their Goddess were they, that none saw Will approach with the dagger. He had retrieved it while they tended to Maeve. Now he waived it wildly. He wasn't aiming it at any of them, but rather drawing with it in the open space of the orchard.

At that moment, Tara Kay remembered.

"*Fuck you, assholes! I'm going to kick the shit out of you cocksuckers!*" *A steady stream of obscenities had started pouring out of Tara Kay's mouth as soon as the SOFE had bound her and had not stopped since.* "*Dry it up*", *she commanded. The girl beside her was crying. Worthless fucking water witches, Kay thought.*

Why had she evaded the tracking spell? She had known it was in that tea Ingrid had given her. She was angry with herself. If she got out of this, she was going to give up her stubborn ways. She might even go beg the Abbess to forgive her and take her back. But those were thoughts for another time. Right now, she really needed to get away.

She looked at her legs again for the hundredth time. Her feet were sunk down in the soggy earth up to her ankles. The ground was saturated with blood in a large circle around a flat stone. It splashed red up on her legs when the girl on her other side struggled. Good for you, fire witch, she thought. At least she was trying something, even if it was futile.

Their feet wouldn't budge. Well, that wasn't entirely true: she could move forward toward the center, but nothing would make her get closer to that psycho. He was waiving that white and red dagger, dancing around, fighting invisible enemies.

I'm going to get killed by fucking Don Quixote, she thought.

She almost smirked but then something happened. A thin trail of light replaced a spot where the knife had been. She thought it was a falling star at first, but it hadn't gone away. In fact, it grew. Longer and wider, the light coming from it was beautiful. It was calling her. She took a few steps forward before she realized what she was doing and could stop herself.

The gap wasn't growing. It was being pulled open. From the inside. Tara Kay stared as an elongated hand seemingly made of light reached out to her. At first she could only feel elated but then she felt what was really happening. That thing with the glowing hand was pulling from her. She had never felt her magic before, not like a part of her body, but now that it was being taken, she could feel the invisible appendage.

She shrieked as her ability was torn from her.

Tara Kay wanted to throw up. How could she not have recognized what was being set up here? The circle that had taken her powers was just like this. Soaked in blood, hers and the women torn to shreds there, it was perfectly staged. The dagger was brandished by a wild man. Just like in her memory, it snagged on the edge of this reality and tore through the veil. Light poured through the slit and for a moment Kay was filled with euphoria.

A hole opened up under Will's feet, not unlike the one that had killed Montana. He was sucked down a foot and then two. A glowing hand, made of light, reached out of the slice he'd made in the veil and grabbed Will's arm, the one that held the dagger. The two Shinar forces, the one from the other side and Yahwe's, played tug of war with Will's body. He screamed and then he tore in two at the waist, his lower half disappearing into the earth and his top, with a tail of spinal cord, went into the cut along with the dagger.

The tear was now being pulled open from the inside. Tara Kay could see bodies on the other side pushing to get through. The euphoria had passed and panic set in. She thought about how the gap had been closed last time.

The SOFE, *not bound in the blood circle but standing around them watching, began to scream too. Apparently they hadn't known whatever they were letting out was going to take from all of them. Tara Kay could only think one thing. The gods of old wanted what was stolen from them. The thought didn't make any sense to her, but she only had a second to think about its absurdity.*

An angel stepped in front of her, cutting off whatever connection the hand had with everyone. The pain stopped, but she felt weak. The giant man was nude and had his arms and wings out spread eagle. His fingers just barely touched another man doing the same on either side of him. They all stepped forward, closing the circle, their bat-like wings overlapping.

The blood disappeared from around their legs as the angels closed ranks. She was free, but she couldn't leave. She heard singing. No, it was more than that. Every sound she heard was involved. Every breeze, car horn, and cricket was intricately woven into the sound. It was more beautiful than anything she'd ever heard before. The light emanating from the center of the angels brightened, silhouetting them against it, and then it dimmed and died away.

Tara Kay needed a Nephilim circle to close the gap. None of the Nephilim here now were there then. They didn't seem to know what to do. There was no one to stop this. She begged Kiyahwe not to let it happen to her again. She would not survive this time. Tara Kay felt a pull on her power, but it couldn't be torn from her. It was secured to her in a different way. She glanced at Nathalia, still clutching Maeve's body.

Both of the women still fed from each other. They were in beautiful agony. Kay remembered the look on the faces she'd seen on the SOFE in the last circle. The light on the other side could steal their abilities. Tara Kay used her ultrasharp teeth to shred her wrists and then shoved her hands into the fertile soil, enriching her connection to Kiyahwe. She pleaded with Kiyahwe, "Help me close the gap."

The earth in front of her began to shift. A mound grew between them and the glowing light. The dirt grew tall and then took on a humanoid form. When the face formed, it smiled at Kay. Red light shone through the constantly shifting and cracking facade, like seeing lava flowing and cooling underwater. Kiyahwe walked among them.

The differences were not subtle, but it was obvious that Kiyahwe and the Shinar shared the same form at one time. They were all made of glowing life, but though Yahwe shone just as bright, she was more dense. Her flesh was churning, turbulent, like molten magma. The Shinar were not solid, just pure energy. It was the difference between the heat of the earth's core and the sun's plasma. Yahwe was female where the Shinar were without gender. Her hair was long but instead of hanging down her back the way the still day would dictate, it swirled up and around her. It was made of flame and heat waves, some tendrils were blue and some clear, with tips of orange and yellow. The Shinar had no hair but were covered in what looked like solar flares.

Nathalia and Maeve's perceived pain was halted the second Kiyahwe manifested. She put herself between the women and the danger. She moved slowly, closing the distance between her and the tear. Her presence ignited the Shinar fervor. They tried desperately to get through to Her. Their color changed and a blackness grew in their center. It wasn't just a dark spot; it was a black hole. It tugged at Kiyahwe's edges. Some of Her flesh was sucked off, flying through the slit.

Kiyahwe didn't let it hurry Her. She pulled a hair from Her head and used it to meticulously sew up the tear. It wasn't the seam that made the Shinar pull back. It was the song. It came from Kiyahwe's mouth, but it also emanated all around them. It was a woman's voice, the most beautiful imaginable, accompanied by the earth moving under their feet, the most terrifying sound. Grinding earthquakes, rumbling thunder, whistling tornadoes, a roaring fire and a raging river accented Her every word.

Maeve was still unconscious but the two Nephilim and their Sinnis witnessed this tremendous occurrence. It wasn't just sound. The earth moved under them. It split and they could see the water table's upheaval. The sky was filled with cyclones and flashing lightning. Flames consumed trees.

In a flash, it was done. The sky returned to normal, as did the ground. The trees smoldered but the fire died. She spoke in their minds and they were grateful her words were not backed by the earth's rebellion.

We closed the portal they opened using the blood of the mother. They have a vessel and a weapon coated with holy blood. Together the two can be used to cut through the veil anywhere it is weakened by bloodshed and violence. This is a dangerous time for all life on Ki.

Couldn't She just close it up whenever the Shinar tried to come through? She had just now, Tara Kay thought.

Kiyahwe smiled at Kay. She heard her thoughts. *No, My chosen. Ki weighs Me down, anchors Me. It is a small price to pay to be joined with the one I love most. Ki and I are joined as one. Manifesting through Her flesh hurts us both, weakens Us. Much time must pass before We can do that again. If I were to separate from Her, I could deal with the Shinar but My nature, without Ki, would drain life from Her. As it is, I cannot keep from pulling from Nephilim when they travel through me.*

Suddenly all of Eiran's warnings made sense. He warned Nathalia that moving through Her was dangerous. She thought it was because of the addictive nature of tabalu, but it was because of Yahwe. She was Shinar. She fed on life and She had no control over it without Ki's calming influence. Nathalia had so much to ask Her, but this was not the time. Kiyahwe's attention was on Tara Kay. Nathalia did not envy her. What weight must the attentions of a Goddess carry.

Kiyahwe was capable of conversing to all of them at the same time. To Nathalia She said, *Never again should you judge the Akhkharu without the One as you did in the desert. Eitan sealed his fate long ago and so I do not hold his death against you, but it was not the time to die for those on the plateau. You are too quick to anger, too quick to action. That is why Those Who See and Observe chose you. They use your own nature against you, and when they come through, they will take the life you have collected for themselves, and yours with it. They use you to collect so that killing you will bring them much of the power I separated from them. You are not only Their chosen but the first of the sister Fates. If you are with Us, against Those Who See and Observe, you must refrain from taking life. There is a greater battle coming and we will need all the allies we can collect. Akhkharu must be given one more chance to choose righteousness and love.*

To Tara Kay She said, *As to the matter of your birthmark…It is my fault that your Guardian has no way to properly claim you. What I have taken, I can return.* At that a single ruddy golden tear fell from her eye. She caught it in a tendril of hair, a thread of fire, a coil of heat. She held out the gift to the Oldest.

Oren shook his head. "I would serve your vessel." It was never for him to choose though he would have chosen Tara Kay given the opportunity.

The ground under Kay's feet moved her toward Kiyahwe. A wind carried the birthright until it came to rest like a necklace in the hollow between Kay's clavicles. Kay's silent scream rumbled beneath them. The smell of cooking flesh filled the air as the lava gem burned through Kay's flesh. Even after seated, it did not cool. It flowed and rippled.

I am afraid my mark is a burden, but it carries a benefit just as heavy. You carry a bit of me within you. A bit of Kiyahwe will give you an advantage in your battle with the Shinar. It will mark you as claimed. Your blood cannot be used to make another DakuAhu. You will not be cursed to live as a danger to your own kind.

Tara Kay blinked and Kiyahwe cooled. Her molten body began to solidify. A volcanic statue stood before them, forever frozen in Her image. *I am not your only hope. There are others who can repair cuts in the veil between this world and that of the Shinar.*

"Who? Where are they?" Tara Kay blurted out.

Kiyahwe's voice was dim now, like she was talking through a long cave. *I cannot see them. Shielding is their natural gift.* She was gone.

THE HALFBREED whose gift was shielding watched as the First and Kiyahwe's vessel left the site he had so carefully arranged. Their Nephilim followed behind them. One carried the holy mother. He laughed, the sound like a cheese grater to a man's skin. Fox, his last remaining vrykolak, took two steps away. Even his child, so vicious as to think nothing of tearing apart the women the Paion had killed, feared him and rightfully so. His appearance was frightening, and he had a mean streak to match.

He was tall, built like a brick wall. A hairy brick wall. His complexion could only be described as ruddy, probably from the massive amount of blood he consumed. Large bat-like wings tattered and torn, at least twelve feet in wing-span, extended from behind his shoulders. His face was that of a dog, distorted, jaw and lips elongated into a muzzle, teeth stained brown. Most disturbing were his eyes. When he got angry, as he was now, they went totally red, lid to lid and corner to corner. No pupil or iris, they were completely alien with their slight glow.

He held this form at all times. His shield made it impossible for Nephilim to sense him, and difficult for Annu to give them his exact location. He had no reason to hide. He was careful to hover a few inches off of the ground. He couldn't risk making contact with Ki.

He made that sound again deep in his throat. It wasn't an amused laugh. It was frustration. Anger. Determination. He needed to get his hands on the other shield maker. She was his. She lived with the Daughters. Her shield protected them. Even he could not cross if she didn't want him too.

He had hoped they would bring her here. If they had, he would have taken her. He'd watched the whole thing, from the Oldest's rising to Kiyahwe's manifestation, but she'd never come. It was a setback, nothing more.

He leaned over and took his vrykolak by the nape of its neck with his teeth. He carried his child like a wolf moving her pups. Like a pup, the hold forced it to relax. It did not struggle. It hung there. With one strong beat of his wings, they were flying.

The Shinar were able to open the veil. There were numerous sites where the veil was thinned by blood or weakened by violence. That was one thing about humans. There was no shortage of atrocities, the magnitude of which could be used by the Shinar. He just had to find one and wait. They would bring him what he desired.

THE BEING who was William Cunningham before being torn in half, tested his new legs. Near weightless, they made him fast and strong and whole again. The Shinar, though they insisted he not use that name in their presence, had miraculous powers. They were God. Maybe they weren't exactly the Trinity of the bible, but they were the real deal. The bible was filtered through the limited minds of humans, after all. There were bound to be some inaccuracies.

Those Who See and Observe, who refused to take names, Shinar or otherwise, had cared for Will after saving him from the earth witch. So powerful was Tara Kay that Will, in his human life, had thought he loved her. He knew better now. She was demon. Or if not by that name, she was at least the enemy of God, so what did that make her?

Will was now the chosen vessel for Those Who See and Observe. He could open the veil to let them through. He could wield the dagger for them. Once he stained it with the blood of an unclaimed Sinnis, it would be a weapon to match him: unstoppable.

He looked around what seemed to be a nursery. A nursery with walls made of rough-cut stones, no less. The arches and heavy wooden doors with rounded tops screamed catholic mission. He was here to kill Ishtar, the One the humans would worship and the Shinar feared so much. Luckily, she was housed where the veil was thin enough that a human could be pushed through. Those Who See and Observe could not come through here. The blood shed had not been the right kind or in high enough levels, though the blood of the First had almost done it. In addition to that, the shield maker was here. She could easily repair the veil and once that was done, this portal would be dead. The Shinar used it sparingly. Will knew he was the second man to be pushed through.

They had told him that time passed differently in their realm. He didn't know how long it had been on earth while he was with the Shinar. He didn't know where he was but the warm air coming through the window told him it was summer. He approached the bed. They hadn't told him Ishtar would be so small. He should just stab through the small, covered mound but he needed to see. He pulled down the sheet.

It was just a toddler. Two years old, maybe three. The letters above her bed said her name was Genevieve. Will lifted the dagger, ready to murder an innocent and then something happened. He couldn't kill her. He wanted to leave, to run, to never look back. The dagger did not want that. It had a way of getting what it wanted.

His arm lashed out, slicing through the tiny palm resting on the mattress over her dark-haired head.

She screamed.

Will stared at her, at the red that coated the dagger's edge and the red that soaked her blankets. They were an odd texture. The plain unbleached cotton threads, hand woven into a simple fabric seemed out of place in the modern world. Then again, everything in this nursery seemed out of place between the ancient stone walls.

He felt the pull and disappeared back into the tear in the veil he had come through. He was back with Those Who See and Observe, all thoughts of her gone. He hadn't killed her, but the dagger was coated. It was now a DakuAhu. The Shinar would be happy enough that it could be used to kill the halfbreeds.

TITLES & RANKINGS

The Daughters of Women are a worldwide network of covens. Each branch organizes themselves into concentric circles according to hierarchy for ceremonies. The largest exterior circle is made up of the uninitiated. They are new to the group and have taken no vows and may be unsure of their magical powers. Inside that are the Novices. Their power types are known, and they have taken the first step toward being a full sister. Inside that are the Sophomores. Sophomores have been selected as the best of the Novices and have a mentor or sponsor from the next group in. These, referred to as the Inner Circle, are the Primos. There is only one Primo of each magical type at a time. Primos are privy to the Daughters' great mysteries. Only after taking the final vows can a woman step into the inner circle. Then all secrets are revealed. At the center of all the circles there is one or two women of the utmost authority for that branch. If there is only one, she is the Abbess. She can be any type of magic user, but she is the ultimate authority for all women below her. If the branch has a particularly strong member, and if the Abbess chooses, next to her in the center is the highest ranking matchmaker.

It is important to note that not all branches have all types of Primos. If a novice comes to them but there is no Primo at that branch for the same type of magic, then that novice must remain a novice or be shipped to another branch where there is a Primo to train and mentor her.

The Abbess sets the tone for each branch. If the Abbess is distrustful of men, there will be less males or no males allowed to live on the grounds with the Daughters.

RANKINGS IN ORDER OF IMPORTANCE AND POWER, STARTING WITH THE MOST POWERFUL

Abbess

Matchmaker (Vinculum) Primo
*probable but not necessary

Primos

Sophomores

Novices

Uninitiated

A group separate from these but who play an integral part in the lives of the Daughters are the **Holy Capacitors**. These are women who reached and held the position of Primo for a number of years. They sacrifice their lives to serve as a sort of magical power collection system, holding a pool of energy from which Primos can pull to work their greater magics. This is one of the great secrets of the organization. Only Primo level witches know of them.

TYPES OF MAGIC STUDIES: NO PARTICULAR ORDER

VINCULUM literally means the bridge or bond. These are the matchmakers. They do small magics and facilitate "hook-ups" for ceremony or relaxation. Their greater magic makes an unbreakable bond between two people that will drive them to find and recognize each other even if they have never met. A Vinculum finds mates for those who need them. They also build the 'bridge' from that matched couple to the Capacitors, for the purpose of gathering excess sexual energy generated by said couples. Vinculum is the most rare and sought after ability. A very strong Vinculum can mean the rise in power of a branch. In this story, Maeve is a Vinculum Primo, and she is the strongest in known history.

PANACEA means the cure. These are the healers. This group widely varies in magical technique. Camilla is the Panacea Primo of the Austin branch.

INGENIUM means the nature and substance. These are the herbalists or potion makers. Ingrid is the Ingenium Primo.

ANIMAVERTO means to see and understand. This is the seer of the group. They have visions of the future and there is a wide spectrum of types and strengths. Jolie is the Annimaverto Primo.

RENUNTIO means to read and report. These are the psychometrists. They can touch a thing and tell, to varying degrees, the history of the thing. Libby the librarian is the Renuntio Primo.

IUDEX means to judge. These are the mind readers. Elle is the Iudex Primo. She must put her hands on someone's skin to hear their thoughts, but she has little control over it. She hears only the thoughts the exact minute she comes in contact with another person's skin.

VINCO means to master or overcome or vanquish in regards to another person. They are telepathic. These people can broadcast or push their own thoughts, words, or feelings into another mind. Nathalia is a Vinco Primo.

PEREGRINUS is a traveler or pilgrim. They specialize in ethereal projection. They can leave their bodies and travel in an incorporeal state. This is a dangerous ability as once the spirit leaves the body, the body is technically dead. The spirit, without the body to anchor it, is a fickle and easily distracted thing. Alisha is the Peregrinus Primo.

LEVITAS is another title and it means the lightning. It is the one power that is known to randomly pop up without a lineage, and oftentimes, in males.

ACKNOWLEDGMENTS

Big thanks to my editor, Hannah Ryder, for all her help.

I'd like to acknowledge my paternal grandparents. Granddaddy bought all the acres where I ran wild, where my imagination and sense of adventure were born and raised. Grandma showed me magic could be made out of soil and seeds. And, they normalized having pie every day.

ABOUT THE AUTHOR

Natalie Gibson writes novels filled with otherworldly violence, sexuality, and the supernatural, and she enjoys mixing horror, magic, fantasy, and romance into her writing. Her stories always have powerful females who change the world, magical creatures that battle their baser natures, and seriously evil bad guys who don't. When she isn't writing, she enjoys drinking coffee, D&D, and playing card games. She resides in central New York with her family.

CPSIA information can be obtained
at www.ICGtesting.com
Printed in the USA
LVHW091652040122
707839LV00014B/165/J